I0618786

Trail of Misery

Post-Apocalyptic Thriller

Apocalypse Trail

– Book 1-

N.A. Broadley

Angry Eagle Publishing

☐
Dedication:

To Christine, my side-kick sista, who has always believed in me. I love you.

To my husband, Michael. Your endless patience as I worked on this novel.

☐
Acknowledgments:

Wow. So many people have helped me with this book, and my list of thanks is long. It is amazing to me how many jumped in and helped me create this dream and turn it into a reality.

Dorene Stalter and D.J. Cooper, I love you ladies. For your help, your patience with my endless questions, and for your inspiration. You are both great mentors and authors, and I can only strive to one day be as wonderful a writer as both of you. Thank you for not allowing me to give up on this book. I couldn't have done this without you.

Truth Seekers, and you know who you are, thank you. For the endless questions, you've answered and the many times you've read through the slush words as I bounced ideas off of all of you. The inspiration you've all given me to continue with this story...you are my peeps, my brotha's and sista's of the soul. Every one of you has taken a very special place in my heart, and I will forever love all of you.

To Roger Boyenga, thank you, my dearest friend. Thank you for the endless hours of reading as you slogged through the first of many rough drafts. For the words: "Keep going," even as I doubted my own storytelling ability. I am so honored that you were the first to read this evolving story and hung in with me as it went through the many changes it had. Hugs, my friend.

☐

Printed in the United States of America
First Printing, 2019
ISBN 978-1-7326212-2-0
☐

This is a work of fiction. Names, characters, places, and incidents are the product of the author's imagination or used fictionally. Any resemblance to actual events, organizations or persons, living or dead, is entirely coincidental.

This is a work of fiction. No techniques are recommended without proper instruction or safety measures and training. The author nor publisher assumes no liability for any action presumed from this book.
☐

Editorial, cover, and formatting provided through Angry Eagle Publishing.

https://angryeaglepublishing.com

N.A. Broadley

Table of Contents

Trail of Misery

Post-Apocalyptic Thriller

Apocalypse Trail
– Book 1-

N.A. Broadley

Angry Eagle Publishing

N.A. Broadley

Day One:

A sickening warmth spread through her stomach, causing her to gag...the stench of blood filled her nose as she bent and wiped the mess up with a wad of paper towels. Another sob caught in the back of her throat, and she swallowed hard. 'I can't cry, I won't cry!' she moaned to the empty room.

Shards of glass lay scattered across the bloody, white tiled floor. The lighter that had been only moments ago held against her skin, lay on the floor. The sight of it made her wince as she examined the blisters that dotted her arms. The blackened skin; blackened where the flame had burned deeper and deeper. She'd screamed in pain when he'd held the lighter against her. The smell of her own burnt flesh was still clogging her nose and throat.

She didn't remember grabbing the knife from the counter, didn't remember plunging it into him over and over and over. But the result was there in front of her — blood, body, lighter, glass. Her hands, slippery and sticky with blood as she brushed a stray hair from across her face leaving behind a bright swathe of red.

Once done mopping up the blood, she grabbed the broom and ever so gently swept the glass shards into a gray dustpan. Her favorite coffee mug...shattered and dumped in pieces into the trash. So much of her innocence along with it.

She winced as a shard pierced the end of her finger, and she instinctively held the wound to her mouth and tasted the metallic saltiness of it. She sank to her knees and sobbed, her breath hitching as her chest exploded with a pain so intense that she felt it in every cell. She should never have opened the door. She should've never peeked out the window; then her neighbor wouldn't have known she was there, and this wouldn't have happened.

She'd known him. Questions raced through her mind. Had he always been a monster? Or was it the event that changed him?

Moving to the doorway that separated the living room from the kitchen, she paused and ran her hand along the door casing feeling the cold wood against her fingers. Momentarily she paused, her fingers moving over the tiny slash marks mapping her daughter's growth over the years. A sigh that came from the very depths of her broken soul, wracking her body. Warm tears flowed from her eyes and she impatiently wiped them away. She'd cried enough and was amazed that she had any tears left.

The virus. The flu. The world had waited too long, people had not paid attention as they should have. The News reports stating it was just a virulent strain. It struck just before Christmas. Just as quickly as the softly fallen snow that buried everything, the virus spread. And people started dying, by the dozens then tens of dozens. And then it was too late.

She found herself glued to the television daily, leaving hair unwashed and clothes ratty. She was held mesmerized as she watched as town after town, state after state fall to the virus. Images flashing across the television screen showed the southern states in panic as thousands fled. Abandoned cars littered the highways as hordes of refugees looking for a place of safety. The body count soared.

It was then she went out and purchased two guns, a small handgun for her hip and a long gun to sling over her shoulder. She didn't know much about using either of them, but she felt safer just having them. She practiced until she was more comfortable. Her aim wasn't bad; not good, but not horrible. Could she disassemble either gun and put it back together? Hell no. But she could hit what she was aiming at most times.

Reports of chaos made the headlines each day; looting, riots, inner cities being destroyed by fires and destruction as people screamed for answers. Countless numbers of people begged for a cure, while watching their loved ones die.

In the northern states, people holed up in their homes, barricading themselves in and away from the virus, away from winter's fury. Then the power went out and never came back on.

Mitch, her husband, had been the first to

get sick. He began to show symptoms just before the start of Christmas break; his body wasting away as the virus wreaked havoc. The smell of his vomit permeating every room in the house, the diarrhea that left him spent and panting for breath. He lasted just three days. By January he was dead but not before he vomited so hard that he ruptured something inside and the blood began leaking from every orifice on his body.

It hit her daughter, Sarah, in January, and she suffered the same fate as Mitch. Beth had held her all the while crying and praying that she would heal, though her prayers fell on deaf ears. Sarah succumbed just as quickly as her father had. This home, the only sanctuary Beth had ever known, was now a death house. It stank of urine, vomit, and feces. No matter how frantically Beth scrubbed, the odor was forever embedded in the wood and the mortar. First her family, now this man lying sprawled on her kitchen floor. Walking over to the sink, she poured water from a bottle sitting on the counter. She scrubbed furiously at her hands with a vegetable brush, concentrating on her fingernails, where blood had embedded in the cuticles.

Numbly, she moved into the living room and grabbed the flashlight that she kept in a side pocket of her backpack. The room filled with a soft glow when she flicked the switch.

Sitting on the floor, she shrugged her

shoulders into the backpack, and struggling against the weight; stood up. She felt like a pack mule. That is what she'd become. Her backpack contained everything she thought was key to her survival. Herbs and medicines, food, lighters, and stick matches, a camp stove, tent, sleeping bag, and one extra set of clothes, all stuffed haphazardly into her pack. Every pocket was jam-packed with items.

It was funny how when the chips were down those things you thought were important for survival, were not that important. The bookshelves in her house contained books; knickknacks adorned the tabletops, bric-a-brac everywhere. None of it mattered for her survival. What mattered was what was in her backpack.

Satisfied that the flashlight was working she made her way back into the kitchen and stepping lightly over the body, she turned the knobs on the gas stove to high and blew out the flame. A hiss filled her ears as invisible gas flowed out. Smiling, she stepped back and waited a few moments for the invisible gas to fill the kitchen before she backed into the living room, lit a magazine on fire, and carelessly tossed it onto the couch. She felt a calmness, and let herself out into the night where she could once again find solace in the darkness. Without a word she disappeared.

The darkness stole her identity as she

walked silently down the desolate avenue. A cloak that hid her yet couldn't hide the pain that seared in her heart.

She knew nothing. Nothing other than what she had read in the many books.

The authors had taught her through their stories. Not that she'd ever had to practice the skills. But now, regardless of the non-practice, their voices whispered into her ear....Dorene Stalter; keep low, stay silent, blend in, and never go into a gunfight with a knife. DJ Cooper; move quickly and wear good walking boots. Only carry on your back what you will need, and keep your head on a swivel. Expect the unexpected. Just a few of her favorite authors among the many. Dorene Stalter; it is okay to be afraid, and DJ Cooper; think, plan, and execute.

The avenue turned left onto the highway where she haunted the side of the road — a ghost in the night. Her feet stung from the cold snow that came over the top of her boots and soaked her socks. Cold feet were the least of her problems.

She moved closer to the woods in case she had to bolt to safety. She was used to the woods, there she felt the safest. The night loomed before her, the darkness swallowing her into the shadows that flitted in and out from the trees.

Her arms hurt. The burns were screaming and pulsing as her long-sleeved sweat jacket rubbed ever so lightly against them. She should have taken the time to bandage them, but the ghosts had chased her from the house. Sarah, Mitch, her neighbor; all drifting in the shadows of every room, looming, threatening, and begging for her to stay.

She was running. Where? South. She knew that if she had any chance of surviving, she would have to leave the cold north of her home state and look for warmer climates.

The winter had been too hard. She had run out of food, run out of ways to keep her house warm. And run out of being alone. She needed others. She needed those who were more prepared, smarter, and more skilled than she was. She had no clue what she was doing, no idea of how to survive in these times. She was living day to day off of little more than gut reaction.

Were there any places left that would be safe? Could she find other survivors that would maybe let her join them? She'd learned from the authors she'd loved reading that there was a better chance of survival when the numbers were larger. As a loner she didn't feel comfortable looking for a larger group but the realist in her knew her chances of surviving in this new world would be slim to none, without the help of others.

She walked with purpose. Her stride strong, her head down against the gusty April wind that had blown in. Snow drifted gently down onto her shoulders. Her hair, tied up into a ponytail, dripped cold drops of melted snow down into her collar sending chills down her back.

She set out for the woods, for the trails that would bring her away from the towns and cities and deep into the mountain ranges. Her mind drifted as memories ghosted her every step.

She had always loved to hike and even went as far as planning a cross country trek along the Appalachian Trail, known to seasoned hikers as the AT.

Her heart ached with sadness as the memories assaulted her; sitting atop the bed with a map spread out before her and her husband, Mitch's arms cradling her, watching as she plotted her dream course. How his warm breath tickled her neck as he leaned into her. She remembered the excitement of purchasing her new backpack, a bright red one, and slowly adding piece by piece of the gear she would need.

Mitch laughed at her when she started freeze drying meals, researching jump off points along the trail where he would meet up with her and resupply her with foods, gear, and what other things she may need. It had been a dream, which now became a necessity.

The authors were a split camp on what was better, woods or highways, and each had valid reasons for what they suggested she do. Highways would be easier traveling, especially on foot. But it would also leave her vulnerable to other humans. Vulnerable to the dangers of those with violent intentions. Woods and trail hiking would be more difficult but less traveled. The AT terrain was known for some tough hiking, but she would meet fewer people, be almost invisible in the deep woods, and it was just plain safer.

Arguing with the authors had become a part of her thought process. DJ Cooper, was a tough, no-nonsense kind of woman, whereas Dorene Stalter had a softer approach, one that guided her gently but toughly through the mind traps that plagued her. They both gave her situational awareness and a "take no shit" attitude.

"One step more, then another, and another." This was her mantra through the darkness. Her steps making soft thuds on the tar as she wove her way through stalled vehicles. She closed her eyes to the horror in front of her. The dead bodies of those who chose to wait for help inside of their cars. All were bloated and had the vacant hollow stares that almost beckoned the passerby to look, to really look. She avoided looking at them. To look would allow the fear that was already choking her to come to the front and paralyze her. Averting their gaze, she stared straight ahead.

The bodies of those who chose to walk and succumbed to the violence of others, dehydration, starvation, or sickness. The bodies that now littered the highway and the grassy banks on the side of the road were bloated, ravaged, and mangled. "One step more, then another," she moaned softly and plodded on.

Dawn brought its first rays of light cascading over the inky black sky. Her feet were sore and her boots, the ones Mitch had helped her pick out at the local REI store, were pinching uncomfortably against her baby toes.

The large, green and white sign in front of her, told her that she'd made ten miles through the night and that Gorham, NH, was a mere twelve more miles away. To her, it felt like it might as well be a thousand as her body screamed with fatigue. Numb fingers grasped the silver guard rail to steady her as she hopped over. She made her way down an embankment and into the woods. She'd find a natural shelter for the day... somewhere that she could crawl into and hide. Somewhere... away from the perils of the highway above her.

Gazing out over the woods, she spied a deer path and tiredly made her way toward it. Sleep called to her softly as she pushed through the high grass that wet the legs of her pants. She didn't think she'd ever been this tired in her entire life. And hungry. How many hours ago had she last eaten? She struggled through the fatigue in her mind to remember. Had it been yesterday morning, or perhaps the night before? She ticked off the food items she had stored in her pack. Enough for twenty meals. If she was careful and only ate half portions, she could stretch that twenty to forty.

A fallen tree surrounded by brush gave her the shelter she was looking for, and tiredly she crawled under it. The ground was damp, and the smell of rotted leaves filled her nose, making her sneeze. At least it was too early in the season for her to have to worry about the creepy crawling things that often nested under this rot.

The morning was warm, unusual for early spring in NH, so rather than pull out her sleeping bag, she chose instead to slip on an extra jacket. Curling herself into a ball, she closed her eyes and let the waves of sleep wash over her.

Chapter One:

Life is a living nightmare

A scream choked her as she woke with a start. Nightmares. With a shaking hand, she wiped the film of sweat off of her face. She'd been having a lot of nightmares lately.

She scrambled across the leafy floor of the shelter, her knees screamed with pain. She froze, and her breath caught in the back of her throat. Standing there, not two feet from her, was a large German shepherd. Two more feet away from her was her backpack, where of course, she had stashed her gun. Muttering, she kept her eye on the dog.

"Shit!"

A staring stand-off. She curled her hand into a fist and slowly extended her knuckles toward the dog all the while praying that it wouldn't chew her throat out.

"It's okay. I'm not going to hurt you."

The dog lowered its nose and sniffed lightly at her hand then gently licked it. He looked up at her with soft chocolate eyes.

"There you go...good doggy," she crooned softly. Boy or girl? She didn't know yet. She spied a bright red leather collar around its neck and from the collar hung a silver disk about the size of a quarter. She moved a bit closer to read the tiny print.

'Jessie? Is that your name, girl?' The dog's ears perked up, and her tail wagged at the sound of Beth's voice.

"Okay, Jessie. I guess you kind'a scared me a bit there. But I think we're gonna be okay? At least I hope we will."

Moving out into the daylight, she stood up and stretched. She could hear the pop and snap of her joints. She grimaced as she slowly worked the stiffness from her muscles. The air was cold, and light flurries landed softly on her face. It was hard to tell what time it was from the overcast sky. The day was still chilly and gray. She'd felt like she slept most of the day but couldn't be sure. The light was deceiving.

She rummaged through the side pocket of her backpack and pulled out a bottle of water, raised it to her lips drinking the cool liquid deeply. Hunger roiled in her gut, the crampy kind that told her she'd waited too long between meals. The hunger gripped her and she gazed around to evaluate the area; she thought she'd be safe enough to start a small fire and cook some breakfast.

She had a smokeless camp stove that she pulled from one of the side pockets of her pack. With one flick of her lighter, flames roared up and out of the small circular tube. She filled her camp pot with water then set it to boil. While she waited, she stood and rubbed her arms and legs to pull some heat back into them. The dog watched her curiously.

Oatmeal with dried raisins and cranberries bubbled in the small pot. The aroma made her stomach rumble, she removed it from the stove, extinguishing the flame. Her mouth watered, the smell of the hot food was intoxicating, and her stomach clenched in anticipation. The first bite of the hot cereal burnt her tongue, making tears well up in her eyes. The next spoonfull, she pursed her lips and blew to cool it, reminding herself to slow down. Jessie, the dog, sat quietly watching her as she gulped down mouthful after mouthful. She looked up when she heard a soft whine.

"You hungry too, girl?'

She pulled a piece of jerky from a small bag in her backpack and tossed it to the waiting dog. One bite, and it was gone.

"Yeah, I know, it ain't much."

She passed the pot with a few remaining spoonsful of oatmeal to the dog after picking out the fruit and eating those morsels herself. Smiling, she watched as Jessie devoured it in seconds, then looked at her for more.

"I'm sorry girl. That's it."

She moved to her feet and sighed as she rinsed the pot with water from her bottle and put everything back into her pack. Once done, she took inventory of her water. She had two sixteen-ounce bottles that were full and one partial bottle left. She knew in the small town of Gorham she'd cross the Androscoggin River where she could fill her bottles. The water would have to be treated before she could drink it, but that would only take moments to do. It was as simple as adding a drop of bleach and letting it sit for thirty minutes. Yeah, it would taste something horrible, but it would keep her from getting sick from contaminated water. She'd have to go lightly for the next twelve miles to conserve what water she had.

She slung her pack up over her shoulders and grimaced as the straps rubbed tightly against her. She slowly made her way back up to the highway. Nightfall wasn't too far off. She grinned as Jessie, who of her own accord, walked contentedly beside her.

"Well, I guess you'll be my Huckleberry," she said as she looked down at the dog and let her fingers sink into the soft fur behind her ears as she patted her.

She stuck to the frozen embankment on the side of the guard rail as she walked. Darkness and snow enveloped her. The air had taken on a bitter chill as she trudged along mile after mile and her breath came out in puffs of white. Her boots were starting to soak through again, and her feet were almost numb. As much as she hated to, she knew she would have to stop, find shelter and get warm, at least for a few hours otherwise she'd be facing frostbite. Shivering, she hugged herself and cut down a soft slope and into the woods with Jessie right by her side.

"Damn girl! I'm freezing!"

She clenched her teeth as she struggled to stop them from chattering. The dog whined softly as if in agreement. Once she entered the tree line, she found the wind had lessened. Pushing in deeper, she found a sheltered spot from the wind and set up her small tent. She didn't dare start a fire. She knew any light from it would give away her location.

She pulled her sleeping bag from her pack and laid it out then struggled to get out of her wet boots and jacket. Sighing tiredly, she crawled inside. Jessie stretched out beside her, and she snuggled tightly to the dog, gleaning any warmth she could.

"I'm just gonna nap a bit girl," she whispered as she drifted off into an uneasy sleep.

Chapter Two:

Just west of where Beth softly snored, Sarah Terrence, a young girl of sixteen, slipped on the icy path. She worried her lower lip with her teeth and tasted the warmth of salty blood against her tongue. How could her father have done this? Unshed tears stung her eyes, making her head ache. All her life she'd bore the brunt of her father. The slaps... the punches... the abuse in so many other ways, and now this. This, she couldn't even wrap her young mind around

She slipped on the snowy, icy pavement and hit her knees with a jarring thud and pain raced through her legs, deep into her hips. She let her head hang forward in despair, hot tears finally flowed down over her face. A blow from behind followed by a sharp voice and another blow knocked the breath from her and brought her staggering upward.

"You had better move it, girl!'

Frank Desota, or as his friends had called him, Franky, pulled the girl by her hair and pushed her in front of him. Leroy Chevs snickered behind him.

"Bitch ain't worth the trouble there Franky...now is she?"

He scowled and thought for a moment.

Oh yeah, worth the trouble? Sure. When he sank into her, it was well worth the trouble. Then giving the girl a swift kick, he muttered,

"Your daddy didn't do me any favors by trading you for my last bottle of Jim Beam."

Sarah stared straight ahead, not acknowledging either of the men who held her captive. But in her heart, a slow burn of anger raged. It was what it was. No better nor worse than what her father had done to her. In all of her sixteen years, she'd never remembered one kind word, one gentle touch only pain. And the pain was, to her, a minor inconvenience. She was used to the pain.

"My turn tonight, right?" Leroy whined. The sound of his voice grated on Sarah's nerves, and she wanted nothing more than to silence him with a swift kick to his throat.

Franky had been keeping the girl to himself and not sharing as he'd promised. And for the past two nights, all Leroy had been allowed to do was watch.

"Maybe. I'm in a generous kind'a mood, so just maybe boy," Franky said then grinned, his teeth stained yellow from the constant wad of chew that was in his mouth. Sarah bowed her head at hearing this. Another night of rough hands, pain, invasion. But then there would be food, or at least that was what she hoped.

They hadn't been feeding her much. Not enough, anyway. And she was always hungry.

With her dad, at least she was not hungry. He let her eat plenty. Maybe that's why he gave her away. Maybe she had eaten too much? She put one foot in front of the other, following Leroy who was in front of her, being pushed by Franky who was behind her. The snow made her feet tingle with cold, and it felt like little shards of glass as it hit her face. She shivered and went deeper into that place where she felt nothing. She let her eyes stare straight ahead as she let herself get lost in the numb blankness that took over her mind.

"This storm is getting worse. We need to hunker down," Leroy whined as he walked into the bitter wind.

Frank nodded. He was sick of the winter and the constant cold. He should have headed south last year when he and Leroy had talked about it. Before the event, and before everything had gone to shit.

"Yeah. I'm cold and tired."

They both moved at a snail's pace as they made their way to the tree line alongside the highway. He'd hoped to make Gorham by dark, but the storm slowed them. They would have to make camp for the night. That was fine by him. He didn't mind camping, and as he looked at the girl in front of him, his mind was already playing with what he was gonna do with her later on. Smiling, he gazed hungrily at her long, slender legs and let his gaze wander further up.

"Yup, I'll be plenty warm tonight," he mused.

∞

Beth woke to a soft, throaty growl and male voices off in the distance. Alert now, she reached out and placed a gentle hand on Jessie's snout, held her breath and listened.

"Did I tell you to sit?" A harsh voice snapped through the darkness.

"Set up that tent and do it now! I'm cold as fuck waiting on you, bitch!"

She heard what sounded like flesh meeting flesh in a slap. She waited for the cry to follow, but none did. Scrambling, she put her boots on and grabbed her pack and her long gun, getting ready to run. If she had to run, as much as she didn't want to, she'd sacrifice the tent.

"I said, come here! Now!" another angry voice shouted.

It sounded to Beth like they were a few hundred yards away. Her heart raced in panic as fear set in. Drawing a deep breath, she poked her head out of her tent and took a quick look. She could see nothing in the inky blackness. Grabbing her long gun, she crawled from the tent with Jessie right on her heels.

"No girl. You stay!" she whispered as she crawled toward the voices.

From behind a thick stand of brush, shadows of two men and what looked to be a young girl fell in the weak light of the crescent moon. Her heart leaped into her throat as she realized just what was happening.

"I said, come here!"

She watched as one of the men yanked the girl roughly toward him and her stomach twisted with nausea.

"When I tell you something, you'd better fucking move, bitch!" he screamed into her face as he grabbed a handful of her long hair and threw her onto the ground.

Beth watched in horror as the man began unbuttoning his jeans. He was going to rape her. Beth bit down on her lip, her teeth drawing blood, to keep from crying out. Fear shot through her as she huddled behind the bush, helplessly watching. Every cell in her body pulsed with anger and screamed for her to help the young girl. The odds were against her. There were two men and only one of her? Gritting her teeth, she felt a moan escape her lips as she watched in horror while the large man crawled on top of the young girl.

Something in her mind snapped. She was filled with rage as she looked on at the brutality happening in front of her. She knew she could not leave any young girl to this fate. Sucking in a deep breath, she brought her long gun up to her shoulder, swallowed hard, trying to control the rage that pulsed inside her. Bile clawed its way up her throat and a hatred so powerful, it was almost consuming; she squeezed her shaking hands tighter on the gun. Never had she walked away from a fight and she'd be damned if she was gonna start now.

∞

Sarah waited for the pain. She waited for the weight of this pig to crush the breath from her, and as he slammed himself down into her, she stared up at the night sky. His smell, rancid, and cloying filled her nose, and she gagged as she turned her head away. Everything in her screamed to fight, but she knew better. Fighting would only make it worse. Closing her eyes, she let herself drift.

She never saw the bullet that slammed into him. She never saw the way his body jumped then folded as he fell to the ground. She heard Leroy scream in surprise but didn't see him go down either. She was waiting... waiting... waiting as she forced her mind to travel away from what she expected to come. It never happened. The only thing she felt was the cold ground as it crept through her jacket and onto her skin.

∞

Beth stood from her crouched position and took a deep breath to steady her shaking legs. The dog, who had crept up behind her, stood as well.

"Well, I can see you listen well."

She scanned the area for other dangers. Her eyes, wild and searching. Seeing none, she walked over to the girl. Her heart cried pitifully for the little thing curled up on the cold ground, eyes closed tight, blood trickling from her nose and the corner of her mouth where her attacker had hit her. Dirt smeared her face, and Beth gently swiped her hand across it to brush it away.

A coldness swept through her as she looked down upon the man she'd just shot. He was no longer a threat. She cast a glance at the other man who lay moaning and writhing on the ground a few feet away. She was in no hurry to deal with him; he wouldn't be going anywhere. Bending down, her knees popped loudly. She laid a gentle hand on the girl's shoulder and whispered.

"Hey, it's okay. You're safe now."

She was startled when the girl opened her eyes and gazed right into her own. Glass eyes…well, not glass but the color of light blue milky glass, and eerily beautiful.

"What is your name?"
The girl gave her no response.

"Are you hurt? Can you get up?" The girl

nodded and shakily pulled her torn clothes around her and stood.

"My name is Beth."

The girl nodded in response.

"Okay, well, I can see you can stand. I gotta take care of a couple of things here. Why don't you go sit over there," she said as she pointed to a rock, "and give me a few minutes."

The girl looked to where Beth pointed and shuffled her way over to the rock and sat tiredly, Jessie dogged her heels as she followed closely behind her.

Beth walked over to the wounded man writhing on the ground. He squirmed and moaned as his blood stained the freshly fallen snow. Crouching down, she looked straight into his brown eyes. The corner of his mouth turned upward as he grimaced. She felt nothing, and she shook her head sadly.

In her other life, the life before the event, she'd been an EMT. She'd run toward trouble to help save lives never did she think she'd be the one to take a life. But now; now she'd taken three lives in the matter of a few days.

"Help me," the man whispered through a bloody, gurgling breath.

Beth shook her head and smiled coldly. She bent and whispered into the cup of his ear.

"Oh, it's way too late for you now, my man!"

Her bullet had hit him to the left side of

his chest. As she looked at the hole, she could see that it wouldn't be long before his lungs filled with blood. Pink, frothy bubbles foamed through the wound as he struggled to breathe in and out. She should let him die in his own time, which wouldn't be long, and save herself the wasting of a bullet. The fact of the matter was that he deserved to suffer. He deserved so much more pain than what her one bullet inflicted. He would have spared that little girl over there no amount of pain, so why should she take pity and save him from the pain her bullet would cause?

"Don't do that. Put that miserable excuse for a human being out of his misery," Dorene Stalter's voice whispered deep in her mind. Placing the barrel of her long gun between his eyes, she pulled the trigger. Gagging, she turned her head and cried as the burning bile rose in her throat, and she threw up on the ground.

Her eyes focused on the chunky white matter that had splattered on her boots. Bits of the brain, bloody flesh, and bone. Wiping a hand across her mouth, she turned and walked back to the girl.

She was sitting on the rock and visibly shivering from the cold. And it was no wonder. She had only a light spring jacket. Walking over to one of the dead men, Beth bent down and with a grunt struggled to remove his jacket. With a hand full of snow, she scrubbed the blood from the front of it and then handed it to the young girl.

"Here honey, put this on over your jacket."

The girl quickly wrapped herself into it. It was far too large for her, but it would keep her from freezing. In the jacket pocket was a pair of warm winter gloves and Beth watched as she slipped those over her hands. She cast a grateful look toward Beth.

"Okay, we need to see what gear and items these two have that we can use,"

She made her way through one of the rucksacks on the ground near the tent. Both of the men had handguns, she took those and shoved them into her backpack. In one of the rucksacks were several items of food, a few cans of soda, a bottle of whiskey, matches, a bottle of water and extra bullets.

The other rucksack contained similar items along with a large buck knife. Beth divided up contents, placing some in her backpack and some into one of the rucksacks that she'd give to the girl to carry. It was a good stash, and it would help her on her journey. She walked back over to the girl, who had been watching her intently, and crouched down in front of her. The miles of walking and the bending sent an explosion of hot, white pain through her knees. She pushed it away.

"Your choice, you can come with me or go on your own with this extra backpack. "

The girl nodded, grabbed the rucksack and slung it over her thin shoulders and stood silently intent on joining her.

Beth smiled. "Okay, well I guess then we'll be traveling partners."

The three of them, Beth, Jessie and the girl with no name, made their way quietly through the snowy woods back to where Beth's tent was set up. It was time to move again. Tiredly, Beth pulled her tent down. She didn't feel quite so lonely anymore.

She led the way while the girl followed silently behind with Jessie bouncing back and forth between them. She hoped to make Gorham by daybreak, then, a quick hike across town to the trailhead that would lead them directly onto the AT. Up higher on the trail, she would feel much safer than down here on the highway.

A bright moon cast shadows on the newly fallen snow, giving the night an almost magical glow. They stopped at each car they came upon, ransacking it for supplies. In one of the cars, she'd found a can of Alpo dog food. Its bright red label with the image of a dog on the front made Beth laugh. Memories of better times flitted quickly across her mind, and her breath caught in the back of her throat as a longing brought tears to her eyes.   Alpo, the normalization of a society that once was. Grabbing the can, she shoved it in her pack. Jessie would have a feast later in the morning when they set up camp.

As she put one foot in front of the other, she glanced every so often to the young girl behind her. She was pretty, with long dark, auburn hair and glass blue eyes. What was her story? Her name? Was the muteness an after effect of the trauma she'd experienced with the two men? Or had she been born mute? So many questions.

The girl was tough; she'd give her that. They'd traveled miles through the snow and cold, and yet not one whimper from her. Her own feet were cold and wet, and she could only imagine how the girl's feet felt. She had only sneakers on, and those were tattered rags at best.

Beth had checked several dead people in the stranded cars, but no one was wearing boots that would fit the girl. She prayed they would find one that wore a size six soon. Yeah, pulling boots off of a dead person was not her idea of a good time, but a necessity was a necessity. The girl would not be able to trek up over the terrain of the AT in sneakers. Her feet would resemble ground meat after only a day or two of wet, icy hiking, which would only slow them down. Boots were a high priority on her list of things to scavenge.

As the first light of dawn filtered through the darkness, Beth struggled with fatigue. Her mind was foggy, and her thoughts jumbled. Her eyelids felt like weights were pulling them down. She was cold, hungry, and tired. All she wanted was a good solid few hours of sleep snuggled deep down into her sleeping bag where the warmth would chase away the chill that wracked her body. Although hungry, food would wait until she woke.

She stumbled as she veered off the road and came down hard on one knee. Swearing, she picked herself up and fought back the tears as she climbed over the guard rail. Trudging through the snow, she cut a path into the thick woods. The girl and Jessie followed slowly behind her as she struggled to bushwhack her way through heavy brush. Leading them deep into the woods, she secured a sheltered spot to set up camp beneath a grove of Pine trees. The air was still and fragrant with the sharp scent of pine. Turning to the girl, she smiled tiredly. Exhaustion was etched deep into her face, and the silence broken by the sound of her sigh as she threw her pack onto the ground with a thud.

"Okay Baby Girl, time for some rest."

Silently the young girl helped her quickly set up the two-person tent. Beth watched her as she quickly and efficiently worked as if she'd done this very thing many, many times. Someone had taught her well.

"I think you've camped a lot during your life, eh?"

The young girl cast her a glance and nodded. Her eyes, that glassy light blue, drew

Beth in and what she saw in them was pain, sadness, and despair.

"I think you've probably been through a lot. More than what I can imagine."

Again the young girl nodded. Then turning her back, she crawled into the tent and laid on the cold floor, hugging her jacket tightly around herself. Beth crawled in behind her.

"No, you will be warm," she said as she laid out her sleeping bag and motioned for the girl to crawl into it. There was plenty of room for both of them, and the shared body heat would keep them both comfortable. The girl looked at her cautiously.

"Don't worry. We'll be safe," she said as she held up her handgun and waved it carelessly in the air. The girl nodded and quickly crawled into the sleeping bag. Beth heard a soft sigh escape her lips as she snuggled down and closed her eyes. She guessed it was probably the first warm, safe sleep this girl had seen in quite some time.

∞

Sarah stared into the gray light long after the woman Beth, had fallen asleep beside her. It was confusing. Why had Beth risked her own life to help her? No one had ever done that for her before. Not her father, not her mother, no one. A shiver ran through her as she thought of the two men who had taken possession of her. Hatred seethed in her throat, burning as she swallowed it down, and she tensed as memories of the first few nights with them flooded her mind. Tears burned at the back of her eyes as she clamped her teeth down on her lower lip to stifle the sobs that threatened to turn into silent screams. Shame covered her. What they had done, what they had made her do….

Possession. An ugly word. It seemed she had always belonged to someone else. Never to herself. Those two men her father had so easily handed her over to? Her father had done a lot of bad things, horrible things to her in the past years but she'd never thought he'd do that. Sell her like a used toy for someone else to play with.

She hugged her arms around her stomach and sobbed silently. It had always been easy to distance herself from the physical pain, but she'd never been able to get away from the pain that was buried deep in her heart. She felt a light touch as the woman, Beth, stroked her hair.

"It's okay baby; it's okay," she heard as Beth whispered to her. Sighing sadly, she wiggled deeper into the sleeping bag and closed her eyes.

Chapter Three:

Beth woke to the sound of birds, the heavy scent of pine and the soft breathing of the girl buried deep in the sleeping bag beside her. Bright sunshine beat down on the tent, giving it a greenhouse effect.

Disoriented and trying not to wake the girl, she quietly crept out of the warmth of the sleeping bag and goosebumps rose on her bare arms from the chilly morning air as she made her way out of the tent.

She stretched the kinks out of her body and looked around. The sun's angle in the sky told her it was morning. They'd slept through yesterday and last night. Jessie, who had silently followed her out of the tent, stood beside her, panting lightly.

"Well, girl," she murmured as she swept a hand along the soft fur of her shoulders. Hunger growled noisily in her stomach as she went a bit off into the woods to pee. She noticed her urine was a dark, tea colored stream; it smelled, strong enough so that it almost made her gag. She hadn't been hydrating enough. Today she would force a couple of big bottles of water into herself. Dehydration could and would lay a person low fast.

As she walked back to camp, she gathered an armful of branches. She'd played with the idea of having a campfire. On the one hand, with a good campfire, she could boil snow for water to bathe in, which she sorely needed. She could hardly stand the pungent, sweaty smell of herself, and she could use the fire to cook a good meal on, which both she and Sarah needed. It would also chase away the chill of the spring air while they waited for nightfall.

On the other hand, it could be a dangerous idea. Smoke from the fire would drift and alert anyone in the area to her whereabouts.

Was it worth the potential danger it might bring? She went back and forth, trying to decide and decided yes, it was a chance worth taking.

She dug through the snow to the ground beneath and laid dried twigs over her fire starting material. Memories of Mitch laughing at her as he watched her construct materials for making a fire jolted her with heartache. She missed him. She missed her daughter. And she missed her life before the event. So much so that she wondered if death wouldn't have been better.

After both Mitch and her daughter Sarah had died, she'd contemplated suicide. She'd put her gun to her head, but at the last minute, she found she wasn't courageous enough to pull the trigger.

As she remembered that dark day, she

shuddered. Recalling just how close she'd come to death with the cold barrel of that gun pressed firmly against her temple. With death, she would've felt nothing. She wouldn't have felt the fear, the loneliness, or the hopelessness that covered her like a heavy blanket. Shaking her head, she pulled herself out of the gloominess that made her want to sit and cry. Crying never did anyone any good. She instead focused her energy on getting the fire started. The memories of how she had made the fire starters brought a sad smile to her lips. She hadn't had any experience. Just what she'd learned from the authors. She had gathered the supplies; cotton balls, Vaseline, nail polish remover, and cardboard egg carton crates. With scissors, she cut the egg carton crates into little individual nests, then covered the cotton balls with Vaseline and a splash of nail polish remover. These she stuffed into a Ziplock baggie. One little nest would start a good fire. She'd made a few dozen of these to fill one pocket of her backpack.

She filled the pan with snow and set it on one corner of the fire pit, where it would melt and warm. In another small pot, she poured bottled water for coffee and set it off to the opposite side of the fire. A bath and a cup of coffee would make her feel new again. She smiled as she looked up to see Baby Girl move up beside her.

"Good morning. We'll have coffee soon."

Baby Girl nodded and sat on a log that Beth had dragged over. Beth watched her as she peeled off her socks. She gasped in shock as she saw the deep, opened raw blisters on her feet.

"Dang, Baby Girl! That is not good! Why didn't you tell me?"

Baby Girl grimaced, and Beth shook her head.

"Okay, well this changes things a bit. The first order of business is to take care of those wounds."

She pulled a baggie from her backpack and opened it to access various smaller baggies containing dried herbs. The bath she had in mind was out of the question now. She would use the water she'd planned for that to make an herbal wash for Baby Girl's feet.

Digging through various bags, she pulled out the herbs she would need. Calendula, Comfrey Leaf, and St. Johns' Wort were great for healing and soothing. She threw a measure of each herb into the pot of water and let it simmer. Soon the air was filled with a pungent and sweet odor as the herbs simmered in the pot.

While waiting on the tea wash, she dug into another pocket of her pack and pulled out a tin of wound heal salve. She spent the next ten minutes cleaning each blister and then slathering on the salve. She produced an extra pair of wool socks she'd packed in her backpack and handed them to the girl.

"Here, these are dry and clean. You can put these clean ones on and throw those rags away," she said, speaking of the tattered and ripped socks the girl had been wearing.

To help with taking the girl's mind off of the pain, she reached into her backpack and pulled out an iPod. Although the world had gone to shit, at least that still worked. And Mitch had bought her a solar charger long before the world or she should say, her world, imploded.

Music might make this process a bit easier though she doubted the young girl would like her choice of music. She had a playlist that included, One Tin Soldier by Tim Selbe, Sad Eyes by Robert John, Mr. Bojangles by the Nitty Gritty Dirt Band among hundreds of other songs she had loaded. Music. The one sanity in an insane world.

Turning it on, she helped Sarah place the earbuds in her ears and watched as her eyes lit up with joy. It was the first expression of emotion she'd seen in the two days with this girl, and it warmed her heart.

Quickly and expertly, she tended to Sarah's wounds; bloody, pus-filled blisters that had broken open. The rubbing of her shoes had opened each blister; the tissue underneath resembling something which looked like raw hamburger. How this girl had walked all these miles with such damage to her feet, amazed

Beth. Not one whimper of pain, not one stumble. It gave her a good indication of how tough Sarah was.

"I wish I knew your name," she murmured as she finished up and rinsed her hands with a bit of warm water. To her surprise, Baby Girl smiled tentatively back at her and grabbed a twig from the ground. She then began to write her name in the snow.

"Sarah."

Beth felt a punch to her heart that took her breath away. She fell back and looked up at the girl with tears forming in the back of her eyes.

"That was my daughter's name," she whispered.

A soft, throaty growl from Jessie alerted her to the danger. Looking up, she stared into the faces of three men. So intent in her work, she hadn't heard them enter the camp. Reaching for the gun on her hip, one of the men shook his head and grimaced.

"Uh-uh Miss, don't do that."

She moved her hand slowly to her side as fear rose up in her throat like a bitter acid. Her shoulders tensed, and she backed toward Sarah, shielding her with her own body.

"We don't have anything Mister. Just leave us be."

The three men stood quietly. The one who had spoken looked sideways at the other two.

His green eyes were sending a silent message. With a nod, he looked at the dog.

"Will that beast attack?"

Beth shook her head and reached out a shaking hand to calm Jessie, who had placed herself between Beth and the men.

"No."

"Good, we are not here to harm you. We happen to be traveling the same path as you. We smelled the campfire smoke and came to see what was going on." The man said as he stepped closer and held out a hand. Beth could feel Jessie's muscles along her back tighten and tense, and she grabbed at the fur along her neck, ignoring the man's outstretched hand.

"Girl! It's okay," she murmured.

"The name is Jim, and this here is Elroy and Carver," the man said softly then smiled. He appeared friendly but so did her neighbor when he had attacked her.

Beth nodded.

Where ya ladies headed?" Jim asked.

Beth took a step to the left blocking Sarah completely from the men.

"We're headed south."

The man, Jim, laughed softly.

"South? Ya girls got quite the walk ahead of you if you're trying to outrun this cold." Then turning to his friends, he motioned for them to check the tent.

"Nothing against you missy but I don't

want someone taking a bead on us from within."
Beth grimaced. He and the other two would see
that she and Sarah were alone. Would they
decide to turn this friendly little encounter into
something more dangerous?

"My husband and a few others are out
hunting. They should be back anytime," she
stammered. Maybe if they thought there were
others, they would think twice about staying
very long.

"Mmmmm…I don't think so, but good
try," Jim replied. He'd scouted the woods before
entering the camp. He knew, if anything, there
were just the two women, the dog and perhaps
someone else sleeping in the tent. He could see
the nervousness in the woman's face — the fear.

"As I said, I'm not here to hurt you. I am
just checking things out. My boys and I will be
on our way. We've got more important business
to do but let me give you a word of advice," he
said tiredly.

"You need to keep a better eye on your
surroundings. Some nasty people are crawling
around in these woods. This time you were
lucky. Next time you might not be. Just a
warning, Miss," he finished. Turning, he
motioned for the other two to follow but then
stopped and turned back to Beth.

"You don't happen to have any antibiotics
in your bag there, do you?"

Beth looked at him. She did. But she

wasn't about to tell him that.

"Is someone sick?" she asked.

Jim nodded, and a quick expression of worry flitted across his face.

"Yes, my wife Mia. She got a nasty cut on her leg a week or so ago. It's infected, and I'm headed to town to see if I can find medicine."

Beth nodded. She was torn between offering help or just minding her own business and letting these men go on their way while she and Sarah went on theirs. Sighing, she looked at Jim.

"How far away is your wife?"

"We've got a cabin about two miles from here, just down over the valley."

She sighed in resolution; she couldn't leave the sick woman any more than she could the young girl.

"I've got medicine and field training as an EMT. Let me see what I can do for her."

Jim's face sagged with relief, and he gave Beth a nod.

"Thank you, Miss. Thank you."

Chapter Four

A brief two-mile walk brought them to a blacktop two-lane road that led to a single-story house. Thick woods surrounded it at the end of the long dirt driveway. On the edge of the wood line were two campers. One blue and white, the other tan and white. Both had awnings that kept them shaded. In another time, this would have been a comforting scene. Something you'd expect to see for a Fourth of July gathering. Now, it was different. It had a desperate feel and look to it.

"Home," Jim said then whistled.

One long burst of sound followed by one short. Beth assumed it was a call to those inside the house. She gazed around, and she saw what looked to be an outhouse toward the back. To the left side of the house, a camp circle with a fire pit in the middle for cooking. The windows of the house had been covered with boards, which helped protect them but also kept any natural light from entering. The scene that spread out before her made her sad. Hiding away, hunkering down, desperate families banding together. Was this the new life they all faced?

There were three large water collection

barrels lined up against the front porch and a wood pile on the other side. Lifting her eyes, she saw what she thought were platforms in several surrounding trees and shot a glance at Jim.

"Look out platforms," he said, answering her question before she could ask. "We've run into a bit of trouble here and there over the past few months."

Beth nodded. Trouble she understood. She'd had more than a bit of it herself.

"C' mon, let's go see how Mia's doing."

Following him up the rickety front steps to the house, she was surprised when two teenagers quickly opened the door. A pretty girl of about thirteen stepped out with a worried expression on her young face.

"Dad. Thank God you're back. Mom's been calling out for you since you left."

Jim, dropped his backpack on the porch, hurried through the door and into the house and Beth followed quickly. Down a long dark hallway that smelled of mold, and something rancid. He stopped at a door she assumed to be the bedroom.

When he opened it, she took a step back from the stench that hit her face. Gagging, she swallowed hard as tears stung her eyes. On the bed lay a tiny woman with dark hair and sunken eyes. One hand, skeletal and twisted, clenching into a fist, hung over the edge of the bed. She was wrapped and tangled in a pile of blankets.

Beth watched as Jim knelt beside the bed and stroked his wife's fevered brow and murmured to her.

"Mia honey, Mia I'm here."

He turned to his daughter.

"Ellie, go get me a glass of water." But the young girl stood frozen, staring at her mother. "Ellie, water… okay?"

Ellie nodded and swept past Beth.

Stench cloyed Beth's nose as she gazed around the room: shadows and darkness. No light showed through the boarded-up window above the bed nor from the other window across the room. It was dank, cold, and the air was thick with the smell of sickness.

She walked over to the bed and bending down; she laid a hand on Mia's brow. It was hot with fever. Turning to Jim, she nudged his shoulder lightly to get his attention.

"Jim, listen to me. I need you to go and boil some water. I also need you to take a board off of one of these windows and get some fresh air into this room."

He nodded and stood up. She saw a mixture of pain and helplessness on his face, and she smiled slightly.

"Don't worry."

A weak smile touched his lips.

"What else do you need?"

Thinking quickly, she counted out the items she would need.

"Water. Boiled water. I can smell the infection. The first thing I need to do is wash the wound and get a good look at what I'm up against. Has she been taking in any fluids? Has she been eating? How long has she been like this? Are you giving her aspirin or Tylenol for the fever?"

Jim thought for a moment before answering.

"She's been sick for about a week now. At first, she just complained she felt weak and tired, then later a bad headache. It was two days ago the fever came on and then yesterday she became delirious. We ran out of Tylenol a while back. I couldn't get any water into her yesterday at all and none yet today."

Beth thought for a moment, chewing on her fingernail as worry wrinkled her brow. Dehydration, lack of electrolytes and minerals… Broth, that's what she needed.

"Okay, do you have any meat with the bone in it?" Beth asked.

Jim nodded. They had just butchered one of their roosters yesterday; he knew there was a bit left of it.

"We need to make some bone broth. It has minerals in it that she," motioning to Mia, "needs. It also has proteins and fats, which will help boost her energy to fight off this infection. Can you have one of the others start boiling the leftover bird down in a big pot of water?"

All the while she talked, she straightened the blankets on the bed and pulled them down on one side to expose Mia's swollen and pasty leg. The injury was mid-shin; an angry red abscess, approximately the size of a golf ball had formed around the wound. Another wave of noxious odor hit her as she bent to get a closer look and bile rose in her throat. Stifling a gag, she swallowed hard. She would have to lance the abscess, clean it out, and insert a wick into the wound so it could continue to drain.

"I'm also going to need you to wet down several towels with cool water. We need to get this fever down."

Jim nodded and set off to do what Beth had instructed. Sarah stood in the doorway, watching her with Jessie by her side.

"Sarah honey, do you remember which herbs I pulled out of my bag for your feet this morning?"

Sarah nodded.

"Okay, I'm gonna need you to get those little baggies. Out of each one I want you to take a spoonful and put into the water that Jim is setting on to boil. Can you do that for me?"

Sarah nodded again, then turned and made her way back out of the room with Jessie padding quietly behind her. Beth took a deep, calming breath to settle her racing heart and stop the shaking of her hands. She could do this. She'd done similar procedures many times before.

She needed a good antibacterial and antimicrobial wound wash, the same combination she'd used earlier that morning on Sarah's feet.

While they were gone, she opened the dresser drawers and was rummaging through them looking for a clean nighty for Mia. She jumped when she heard an angry voice behind her.

"What are you doing in my mom's dresser?"

Turning, she glanced over at a young boy who was standing in the doorway. His face darkened with a scowl, and his eyes flashed anger and worry.

"Your mom needs to have a change of clothes. Hers are dirty, and they smell."

The boy walked quickly to the dresser, pulled open the third drawer, and pulled out a nightgown, and handed it to her. He then looked up at her with tears in his eyes.

"Can you help my mom?"

Sighing, she nodded. She didn't want to lie to the kid, but she also didn't want to give him false hope. The woman was sick, probably dying. She'd do what she could, but she wasn't a doctor, and this was no sterilized hospital room.

"I'm sure gonna try kiddo."

She turned back to the bed and began

undressing Mia while the boy stood off to the side and averted his eyes.

"What's your name, kiddo?"

"Bobby."

"Well, Bobby, I'm gonna need your help. Can you find me some clean sheets for your mom's bed?"

He nodded and grinned. Happy to be helping he ran from the room hollering to Ellie to help him get the sheets from the top shelf in the hall closet and zipping past his father who was carrying a pan full of hot, herbed laced water, and wet towels into the bedroom.

"Woah slugger! Slow down," Jim said as he sidestepped the boy. Beth heard what sounded like splintering wood as the boards came off of the window above the head of the bed. She looked up to see Carvers face staring in at her as light flooded the room. Beside him stood a woman who Beth guessed to be in her thirties, smiling through the space at her.

"Hi, I'm Jill." The woman said softly. "I'll be in to help you in a minute."

Beth smiled and nodded. The helping hand would be great.

"I hope you don't have a weak stomach." The stench in the room was almost suffocating; sweet, thick, and cloying. She could almost taste the odor in the back of her throat, and it made her want to gag.

Now that she had more light she could

see the wound on Mia's leg. What she saw took her breath away. Greenish, thick pus mixed with the red tinge of blood oozed from an inch-long gash that ran longwise to her shin bone. This area was swollen and bright red where the abscess had formed. Above and below the wound, and surrounding the abscess, the leg was bright red and dappled; indicating that cellulitis had set in.

It was quite an angry infection. She also suspected that Mia was experiencing sepsis, a condition where the infection had spread to her bloodstream and was now traveling through her body. All this from a simple scratch on her leg.

She watched as Jim laid the pan of boiling herb infused water on the bedside table and looked down at his wife's leg and cringed. Sarah and Jessie stood in the doorway, neither daring to come further into the room and the nauseating stench of sickness.

"It's bad, isn't it?"

She nodded and looked at him bleakly.

"Yes."

"Can you help her?"

"I'll do my best, but I think this infection has traveled. Have you ever heard of Septicemia?"

He nodded. He had. He'd seen it first-hand with his father. But when his dad had gotten sick with it, there had been hospitals, medicine, doctors to treat him. And even then, they'd almost lost the old man.

"Her infection has gone so far, Jim. I don't know if the antibiotics I have will kick it out of her," she murmured sadly.

He looked at her desperately. His voice hoarse with emotion that made Beth want to cry.

"You've got to try. I can't lose her."

She nodded. She would do everything she knew to help Mia, but she wasn't a doctor.

She set to work now that she could see what she was doing and began to wash the wound, continuously draping wet towels over Mia's fevered body.

Sarah stood at the doorway and watched her intently. The medicinal tea had cooled enough where she could dip the washcloth into it without burning her fingers or Mia's skin. The crusted puss and blood sloughed away easily exposing the nasty gash which had begun to close up on its own. Hearing a whisper, she looked up to see Jill talking to Jim.

"What can I do to help?" she asked as she moved over beside Beth. "I don't have any medical experience I'm sorry to say. But I can follow orders well."

Beth smiled and pointed to her backpack on the floor.

"I need the scalpel from my backpack," Beth replied, explaining that she was going to have to reopen the wound to debride it. Jill quickly moved to where Jim had set Beth's pack down and began to dig through the pocket containing her medical kit.

"Okay got it."

"I need you to sterilize it," she said. Turning to Jim, she asked, "Is there any alcohol in the house?"

"Yeah, there's a bottle in the bathroom. I'll get it."

Looking at Sarah, Beth grimaced.

"Honey, you may not want to watch this."

Sarah shook her head. She didn't want to watch, but she was too terrified to leave Beth.

"Why don't you go and help with the chicken broth?" Beth suggested. She knew Jim had asked Ellie to get it started and Carver was out tending to the fire it was cooking over. She saw a worried expression cross Sarah's face.

"Don't worry, honey. These people won't hurt you," she assured her.

Jill turned and smiled warmly at the young girl.

"You betcha they won't, or they'll have to answer to me," she quipped, trying to set the girl's mind at ease. She had noticed Sarah appeared very timid, fearful, and shy. She couldn't say she blamed her. Every day she was fearful. Since the event, it seemed that they all had taken fear as their daily companion.

Jim brought back the sterilized scalpel and stood wringing his hands as Jill assisted by holding Mia's leg still. Beth grit her teeth, sucked in a deep breath, and steadily sunk the scalpel into the wound. Making an incision the full length of it, opening it back up. She watched as an explosion of putrid, green pus, and blood poured from the area. Gagging, Jill turned her head and Jim, unable to watch, hastily exited the room. Mia moaned and began writhing with pain.

"Hold her tight," Beth growled as she began to scrape away the dead and infected flesh. The wound ran deep and bled freely. She packed a strip of gauze into the incision and left a tail of it sticking out; a wick of sorts for the infection to flow out through. Washing away the blood, she then placed a light bandage over the area, and Mia settled back down.

Sighing tiredly, Beth sat back on the balls of her feet.

"Okay, the worst of it's done. Now we need to give her some antibiotics and hope the hell it will be enough."

Digging through her pack, she pulled out seven large brown bottles of antibiotics. Each bottle contained five hundred doses. Jill looked at her questioningly.

"I used to work part-time at a hospital. When the shit started to go south, I broke into the medical supply closet and just grabbed whatever I could get my hands on."

She sorted through the bottles looking for

the best one to treat Mia. She would start her on Rocephin, a powerful broad-spectrum antibiotic that she knew would give Mia the best chance of kicking out the infection. If that didn't work, she still had six more in her arsenal to try. She had Ampicillin, Amoxicillin, Doxycycline, Penicillin, Ciprofloxacin, and Azithromycin. One of them would surely have to help.

She had Jill hold Mia in an upright position while she spooned a couple of crushed pills into her mouth then gave her a spoon of water to wash it down. She rubbed the front of Mia's throat gently as the woman coughed weakly trying to swallow. After they laid her back down, she stood, placed her hands on her lower back and stretched tiredly.

What she'd done, the procedure to clean out Mia's infection, left her with doubts that it would help. This type of infection needed a doctor, a sterile environment, and this room was far from sterile or even clean. Is this what it had all come too? Medicine and medical procedures that were set back hundreds of years? Because of what? The event. Everything she lived and did today was because of the stupid event! She longed for the life she had before. Having clean hospitals, running water, the abundance of food in the grocery stores, and the comfort and safety of her home and family.

"There's nothing more I can do now."

Jill nodded.

"Okay then, how about I fix you a cup of coffee? We ain't got much here, but the coffee supply is still holding up."

Chapter Five

Jim stood, warming his hands in front of the campfire. He watched as the soup bubbled and boiled in a pot hung suspended on a tripod over the fire. Elroy and Stacy with their little two-year-old Jake, sat on chairs watching Ellie and Bobby as they played boisterously on the tire swing hanging from the old maple in the front yard.

Jim shook his head sadly as he watched the girl, Sarah, standing silently off to the side with her dog, Jessie. He wondered about her. She hadn't spoken a word, not one word. Did she not talk? Was she unable to talk? And those shoes she wore? Nothing but canvas rags held together with shoestrings.

He made a mental note to check Mia's closet to see if she might have a pair of good warm boots for the girl. This thought made him grin. Mia and her shoes. The woman must own hundreds of pairs. It was her quirk, one he often teased her about bringing her to laughter. Shoes and boots of every fashion piled high in her closet and then when she ran out of room in her closet, she took over his closet. Yes, she'd have a pair that he could give to the girl, Sarah.

Carver was stirring the chicken soup with

a wooden spoon and turned, nodding his head at Jim.

"How's Mia?"

"I dunno. Man, I just dunno," Jim replied, his voice heavy with anguish. The woman, Beth, was doing the best she could, that he knew, but his heavy heart whispered that it might not be enough.

"She's pretty sick. Beth was cleaning out her wound and treating it, but I don't know if it'll be enough."

Carver shook his head.

"Have faith, brother. The Lord will see her through this."

Jim nodded and hoped his friend was right. Carver, he knew, had more faith in God than he did. His faith, weak at best, left him wondering about a lot lately. It left him questioning. If God was so great, then why the hell did he allow this rampant disease to spread as quickly as it did? Why did HE sit back and not do anything for the people he supposedly so loved? No, he didn't have much faith. He was pretty pissed off at this so-called Father for all that had happened.

He looked at the pot of soup and thought about their need to hunt again. They were down to twelve chickens left in the coop and the pig they had slaughtered two weeks ago was about gone. Their food supply was dwindling fast. Mia, thank God, had been quite skilled in the kitchen, canning and laying up quite the supply of meats, vegetables, and fruits. This skill had gotten them through the worst of the winter. They would plant the garden in a few short weeks, but they wouldn't have anything from that until fall.

From here on out it would be foraging for berries and hunting to keep them all fed. The store-bought foods they had set by at the beginning of the event was now down to a few meager supplies. Not enough for them all. God, he wished he had been smarter and more prepared. But he, like many others, had not expected this. He had not thought it possible for everything to turn to shit in the matter of a few months.

Beth followed Jill from the room and into a small, dark kitchen where there was a pot of coffee brewing on a small camp stove. While Jill poured them both a cup, Beth sat at the table and wearily closed her eyes. Hunger gnawed at her stomach like a frenzied rat. She hadn't had breakfast, and she guessed it was getting pretty close to noon time. She was sure that Sarah was just as hungry as well.

"I've got to fix Sarah and me something to eat." She said. "Would you mind if I used the stove to cook us up some food?"

Jill smiled as she set a cup of hot coffee in front of Beth.

"Of course not. But I'm betting the guys

have that soup about ready and wouldn't mind sharing. We can pour off some of the broth for Mia and then split the rest among everyone."

Beth nodded gratefully. She would welcome a warm bowl of chicken soup, and she knew Sarah would as well. They had been living for the past two days off of oatmeal and herbal tea. Grabbing her coffee, she followed Jill out into the spring sunshine.

She sat by the fire, the sun warm on her bare arms as she sipped her coffee and listened to the conversation. The chicken soup bubbled, and the fragrant aroma surrounded her, making her mouth water and her stomach growl. It seemed; lately, she was always hungry. Even after she ate, the hunger was still there, like a shadow in a dark alley, waiting and chewing at her.

"I saw some deer sign back by Lalor Ridge when we came across it this morning. We need to start there," Carver said as he threw another log into the fire pit, sending up sparks of embers to float in the air. Jim nodded.

"Yeah but remember, that's close to the Epperson's. You know they ain't gonna take a liking to us hunting in their territory."

Carver grimaced.

"Too bad. It's public property. Those boys don't own that damn mountain." They'd had some trouble with the Epperson boys in the past few months. Just angry words and threats, but times were getting more desperate by the day. Carver had no doubts that the worse things got, the more violent the threats would become; until one day it would escalate out of control. Someone would end up hurt, or worse, dead. They'd managed throughout this winter to keep peace with all their neighbors, but now this peace was tentative at best. They were all getting desperate. Hunting had ravaged the wildlife in the area, and they all were having to go further and further away from home to find even the smallest of game.

As she listened to the conversation, she shook her head. It was like this in her old neighborhood. In the beginning, the neighbors tried to help each other out, thinking that the situation would end, and everyone would be back to normal — kindness as one neighbor after another brought soup and medicine to those neighbors who were sick.

Then once they realized that things were only getting worse and there was no help coming, neighbors began to turn on each other. The stronger, stealing food and supplies from the weaker. It had become nasty and dangerous quickly. People she'd known for years, friends she'd spent summers picnicking and biking with had gone from being nice and polite to downright scary. Her thoughts were interrupted by a soft touch to her shoulder, and she looked up to see Sarah standing beside her.

"What's up kiddo?"

She watched as Sarah touched her stomach.

"Yeah, I'm hungry too. The soup should be just about ready."

As if on cue, Jill hollered, her voice booming for a woman so small, as she motioned for everyone to gather at the picnic table where she had laid out bowls.

"C' mon everyone. Let's get it while it's hot."

Ellie and Bobby jumped from the tire swing and raced to grab their bowls. Stacy, carrying Jake on her hip, quickly followed. Beth grabbed an empty bowl for Sarah and scooped a ladle full of chicken soup into it when she felt Jill move up beside her.

"No, take more than just one ladle. That'll never fill that child's hungry belly."

She looked at her and shook her head.

"No. There's barely enough here to feed all these hungry mouths. I feel bad just taking this," she replied.

Jill scowled and grabbed the ladle from her hand and scooped another helping into the bowl she was holding.

"It's enough. Everyone will get fed. Trust me."

Jill then began dishing soup out for every person. Beth saw that she had also set aside a large bowl of the broth to cool for Mia. Quiet filled the air as everyone settled into eating. It was funny how before the event Beth had thought nothing of tossing the broth from a chicken noodle soup into the drain. Now though, she slurped every last drop from her bowl as if it was the last meal she would ever eat. What she once took for granted was no more. She took nothing for granted — every drop of soup, every morsel of food.

After their meal and some quiet conversation, she looked up at the sky and shook her head. In a few hours, darkness would set in, and she would be on the move again. The thought made her cringe. Her legs were tired, her body ached. Pushing herself up from the table, she pulled Jim aside.

"I'll leave you with enough medicine to get through. You need to follow my instructions and make sure that Mia gets every dose," she explained. Jim nodded.

"Are you leaving?"

She cast her eyes skyward.

"Yeah, we've been traveling at night. It's safer."

"You could stay the night and head out tomorrow," he suggested.

She shook her head. She came to help, and she did. These people had barely enough for themselves, never mind two extra mouths to feed. And besides that, she had an urge to push on. The AT was only a few short miles south of where she was, and if they hustled, they'd be able to make it easily in a few hours.

"No, Jim. I gotta push on," she said softly. "But, I'll leave you with everything you need for Mia. You should see improvement, if there is going to be any, within the next twenty-four hours. My advice to you is to get to the nearest library, find any medical books that are there, books about foraging, plants, herbalism and the like. Study them. Use them. Teach your children."

Jim nodded. There was so much he didn't know. He, like everyone else, had become so dependent on the conveniences of easy living that they gave no thought to what would happen if it all fell apart. That one little *IF*… had turned to certainty as the virus ran its course through America.

"I was lucky to have the medicine Mia needed, but it won't last forever. And we can't make any more like it. So, herbs are gonna be your medicine for the foreseeable future. That tree over there," she said, pointing to a tall and wispy willow, "the bark contains the same medicine that is in aspirin. It will help with pain and fever. Learn to use it and those plants around you," she finished.

Jim nodded. She was right. They needed to learn how to navigate this new world by re-learning old ways. They needed to learn folk medicine, animal husbandry, gardening, and all those things that were left behind and forgotten by many.

"I will. How can I repay you for helping us?" he asked. They didn't have much but if they had what she might need he'd gladly give it for what she'd done for Mia.

"Do you happen to have a pair of size six boots? Sarah is desperate for good boots. Her sneakers are in tatters, and her feet are chewed up with blisters," Beth explained. Jim smiled.

"I do."

Chapter Six

The sun set behind the mountain ridge, and she paused to watch it sink below the horizon. Golden light spilled over the green of the treetops. Gloaming. She remembered a book, or was it a movie she had watched, with that word in the title? It had sounded so romantic at the time. Now, the gloaming meant time to move, quietly and stealthily.

Jessie dog sniffed the ground ahead of her. Sarah followed behind. Boots slapped pavement with each step. Boots, good hiking boots, covered Sarah's tender feet. Warm boots that would hopefully hold up for the journey ahead of them. She had felt a sadness leaving Jim and the group. Sadness and doubt.

Would Jim and his family make it? She guessed their chances would be about as good as her chances of surviving this. She could've stayed. But she cringed at the thought of another cold and snowy winter, at the thought of scavenging for wood, of being cold and hungry all the time. No, going south was the smartest thing to do. Where the climate was warmer there would be no hellish, freezing temperatures or blasting snow and ice storms to deal with.

As darkness set in, their path was lit with

the glow of a weak crescent moon. Shadows danced in and around the trees on the sides of the road. She stood in front of the trail sign. Appalachian Trail. They had made it to the trailhead. On a small wooden brown board were arrows pointing north and south. She would be headed southbound.

Patches of snow and ice mixed with mud covered the narrow path leading upward into the mountains. Doubt filled her as she wondered if she was up to the challenge. A heaviness settled on her heart. A deep sadness almost too much to bear. This was not how she'd imagined entering the trailhead. It was so far from what she had planned. Her husband and her daughter were supposed to be here with her; hugging her and seeing her off on a great adventure. She tensed her shoulders, took a deep breath, and let memories wash over her like a soft silken blanket.

It wasn't supposed to be like this. Leading a mute girl and a dog over a thousand miles through God knew what kind of terrain and dangers. Shaking her head, she glanced over her shoulder to where Sarah stood on the blacktop. She could go back, back to where Jim lived and ask to stay with them. They could use her skills for sure. But she wouldn't do that. Sighing deeply, she motioned for Sarah. As they walked, she talked quietly with Sarah.

"You could have stayed Sarah. They

would have taken care of you."

She felt Sarah grab her shoulder, and she turned and looked at her. The young girl shook her head, vehemently.

Nodding, she understood.

"Time to climb then, girlie."

∞

Sarah followed behind Beth. She let her eyes wander over this woman who had taken her in. She was thin. But then again, everyone was thin these days. And hungry. She thought about Beth telling her she could stay with the family she'd helped. She knew she could have, but something in her told her Beth needed her as much as she needed Beth. Yes, staying with the family would have been easier than hiking along this icy, frozen trail. But somehow she suspected, in the long run, it wouldn't have been better for her.

She liked Beth. She could see a kindness in her eyes. And, she could see that Beth was just as lost as she was. She was looking for a place to make a home. In that, she felt they were two kindred spirits; lost, needing each other.

The pack on her bag weighed heavily on her shoulders, creating a hot and burning pain where the straps rubbed against her tender flesh. Grimacing, she shifted the weight to release some of the pressure. This pain was a mere inconvenience compared to what she'd been through. This pain she could live with. She made a mental note to see if Beth had a swatch of material that she could pad the straps with.

∞

It was late at night, and they were still moving. The sky was as dark as black ink. The crescent moon was dodging in and out from behind clouds. They climbed over rocks the size of Buicks and slipped on the ice as they pounded through the mud and snow; cold and wet. And they'd made three lousy miles. It was disheartening. Dawn was just a few hours away. Beth finally gave into exhaustion, into the coldness, into the freezing water and slush that seeped into her boots. Sitting down on a boulder, she let her shoulders slump in defeat, and sighed tiredly.

"Okay, Baby Girl. I'm done for this night."

Sarah nodded and moved up to sit beside her.

"We'll make camp as soon as we can find a level spot kay?"

She felt rather than saw the relief from Sarah as the girl leaned her body against her. Pushing herself up from the boulder, she moved through the dark praying they wouldn't have to go too much further before they found a suitable spot to set up the tent. She could hear the clicks of Jessie's nails as they scraped against rocks that littered the trail, and those rocks promised a twisted ankle if they weren't careful.

She figured they were far enough up the trail and away from the small town of Gorham, New Hampshire that they'd be safe. Although Gorham had been eerily silent as they passed through, she'd spied some campfires in the distance. She tried to make sure no one had seen them as they skirted the town, but one never knew, and she wasn't taking any chances.

Thus the push to get as far up in the mountains as possible. A person would have to be a fool to have tried to follow them. Besides that, she was confident that had they been followed, Jessie would already have alerted them.

In the weak light of dawn, she quickly set up the tent while Sarah lit the smokeless stove to make breakfast. They ate oatmeal again. The bland taste rolled across her tongue, thickly. It didn't matter. She was too tired to care. Her legs and feet were on fire from the night's exertion of climbing up steep, rock-strewn hills and her shoulders ached from carrying the heavy pack. A burning blister had formed on her baby toe, and the stinging pain reminded her that she would need to tend to it before it got worse.

Gulping down the oatmeal, she crawled into the tent just as the sun rose. Sleep. Hours of rest for her tired body. She looked over at Sarah, who was sharing the sleeping bag with her and smiled. No sooner had the girls head hit the rolled-up jacket used as a makeshift pillow she had fallen asleep. Jessie was stretched out beside them; her furry body pressed tight against Sarah's back.

With a sigh, she let the night ease from her body. Now that they were on the trail and deep into the mountains, she could go back to traveling during the day. Day traveling would be much easier and leave them less prone to accidents.

Thankfully the White Mountain range was behind them as they entered the trail well beyond the treacherous Presidential Range. But the going would still be tough. And hiking at night, well that was just downright foolish and dangerous.

She woke to bright sunshine and bitterly cold temperatures. She could see her breath with each exhale. Judging from the light and the sun angle, she guessed it was just before or just after mid-day. That would give them a good six hours of hiking, which should put them closer to the Massachusetts border. They still had several mountains to traverse, but once past those, the hiking should get easier.

Doubting herself, she shook her head.

Was she crazy for attempting this? Should she go back? Back to what? Back didn't offer anything good. Forward only offered the unknown. Growling in frustration, she poked her head into the tent and called out to Sarah.

"C' mon baby girl. Up and at 'em."

After a quick breakfast of dehydrated cheesy noodles with flakes of dehydrated tuna, she rinsed the cooking pot and tucked it into her pack. Everything tasted like cardboard. Flavorless and uninspiring.

From a nearby stream of snowmelt runoff, she filled two water bottles — one for herself and one for Sarah and added bleach to them. Anxious to put miles under her feet, she set off at a quick pace. Her knees screamed with pain, and she struggled back a moan. How many miles had she done in the past few days?

Walking in daylight, it was much easier to navigate the trail and sidestep the many obstacles. Rocks and branches Lay strewn in all directions from winter storms, icy spots that the sun hadn't yet melted littered the trail. Sweat formed between her shoulders from the exertion and the rubbing of her heavy pack. She could hear Sarah behind her panting as she too struggled. The forest was filled with scents of pungent, sharp pine and the earthiness of rotted leaves. She took a deep breath, tasting the scents on her tongue. She loved the forest and had the situation been different; she would have been enjoying this hike.

Jessie bound ahead, sniffing and exploring. She envied the dog and her seemingly endless amount of energy. A loud snap of a branch breaking to the left of where she stood, brought her to a standstill. Jessie, sensing danger, made her way quickly to Beth's side. Sarah, wide-eyed and frightened, slid behind her. She reached down for the gun on her hip, sliding it slowly from its holster. Holding her breath, she waited and a few seconds later, watched in amazement as a lumbering black bear crossed the trail a few yards ahead of them. It stopped, swayed its big head left then right, sniffed the air and grunted. Beth's heart froze in her chest as fear tightened her gut. She looked at Sarah and with a firm hand, held onto the scruff of Jessie's neck.

"Oh big boy, just mosey along okay?"

As if taking her advice, the bear gave them all one short glance and then bounded off into the thickets. A whooshing breath of relief escaped Beth's lips, and she felt Sarah relax behind her.

"Shit, that was too close."

Sarah smiled shakily, and nodded.

From deep in her mind, where the voices of the authors resided, she heard a chuckle and a whisper from D.J. Cooper.

"That was food, Beth. Good meat to fill your belly and girlfriend? You let it just pass you by."

Beth sighed from the depths of her tired body.

"I think it's time to take a break."

She slung her pack to the ground with a thud and sat down beside it. She could see that Sarah was tired, and she felt a twinge of guilt for pushing her so hard all afternoon. Reaching into her bag, she pulled out two strips of jerky, handing one to Sarah who took two bites in quick succession. The bear came to mind, and with a growl, she shook her head. Sarah looked at her with a queer expression, and Beth just smiled.

"It's nothing. Just a pain in the ass thought."

Sarah answered her with a shrug of her slim shoulders. Beth knew she understood that their food supply was limited, but this didn't make her feel any better. D.J Cooper was right; she should have shot the bear. But then what? She had no idea how to gut it, to skin it, to process any of the meat?

She took several bites of her jerky and with a sigh, tossed the remainder to Jessie, who was sitting patiently at her feet staring up at her.

"Damn! You too? As if I don't feel guilty enough. Why don't you go hunt us down a rabbit or something?" Glancing over at Sarah, she laughed.

"Yeah, you think it's funny? What I

wouldn't give for a rabbit stew right about now."

Sarah nodded her head in agreement and rubbed her stomach for emphasis. Beth stood up and stretched, her sweaty shirt clinging to her body and wrinkled her nose as the musty, sweaty odor that assaulted her nose. She would give her right arm for a warm shower about now, one with sweet smelling lilac soap and shampoo for her hair.

Sighing wistfully she turned to Sarah.

"Okay, we can get a few more miles behind us before dark so let's get our asses in gear."

Chapter Seven

Two more full days of hiking brought them to Massachusetts's border and into the Berkshire Mountains. I-90 was about four miles, down-hill to the left of where she stood, according to her map. She had a decision to make.

Hike down to the highway, scavenge through the cars and trucks to find whatever supplies they could, or travel deeper into the ninety-mile stretch ahead of them and hit the smaller back roads leading to smaller towns.

Chances were that the back roads and small towns would have had less traffic, thus, less stranded vehicles for her to scrounge through. And those they did find on the back roads would probably already be stripped clean of anything worthwhile. Ninety miles of trail before they would enter yet another state, Connecticut. Ninety miles, at roughly ten miles of good hiking a day, would take nine to ten days to cross the Berkshires.

She'd heard this terrain wasn't as treacherous or nearly as difficult as the Whites (the White Mountain Range) and she was praying this was true. They were both getting their hiking legs under them, but those first few days had taken its toll. They both had sore muscles, bruises, exhaustion. They would need a rest day soon. Turning to Sarah, she paused a moment and slid her heavy pack off of her shoulders and set it down on the dirt-packed trail.

"What do you say we stop early today, set up camp and take a good day of rest?"

Sarah nodded as relief spread across her face.

"Yeah, I agree with you baby girl. I'm tired too."

With that, she made her decision. Together they built a nice campfire to chase away the chill and dragged a downed log from the woods to use as a backrest. She dug through her pack and pulled out a bag of dehydrated beef noodles with peas and carrots. She decided they were both going to have full portions, and as she cooked it up over the fire, the scent of it filled her nostrils and made her mouth water. Thoughts of pizza and burgers, of potato salad and steak, teased her as she let the noodles simmer. She pushed the thoughts away with a discouraged grunt.

Resting, leaning back up against a log, relaxing, cooking up a decent meal, hydrating with lots of water sounded like just the thing they both needed. The supplies were taking a hit with having an extra mouth to feed, and although they both had been eating the minimal of one meal a day, she desperately needed to try to find some resupply foods.

One meal a day with the strenuous hiking they were doing was not giving either of them the caloric intake they needed, and she could feel this in the way her clothes hung loosely off her body. She'd lost weight and looking at Sarah; she could see that she had too. Even Jessie dog was looking slimmer. At least the weather had cooperated. Dry, warm spring days and cooler nights but not dipping into the downright cold temps they'd been having.

Looking at the wind-up watch, she wore on her left wrist; she saw that today, May 10th, was her late husband's birthday. God how she missed him and how she missed her daughter. Tears formed like a small bead listing on the bottom lid, waiting for its moment to fall, and with a shaking hand, she wiped them away quickly. That was another life, another lifetime.

After eating, she scouted the woods around them while Sarah dozed by the fire. The first of the spring plants were popping through the cold ground, and she knew of several she could harvest to add with tomorrows meal of dehydrated pasta and cheese.

Early fiddleheads, deep green and leggy sprung up in clusters. Violet, bright purple dotted sunlit grassy areas and bright yellow dandelions, the leaves, stems, and flowers would give them not only fresh food but also pack a punch of vitamins and minerals their bodies needed. Digging her hands into the warm soil, she dug up the dandelions, roots and all. The roots she'd save and dry for tea. Dandelion roots would work well for helping with the diet of dehydrated foods they were on by providing a subtle laxative effect.

While she searched for the spring plants, Jessie dog nosed about the area, digging under fallen logs, chasing squirrels and startling birds. Beth loved the silence of the woods, the earthy aroma that drifted slightly on the breeze. The peacefulness.

And Jessie, full of energy, was always happy no matter the situation. At that moment she found herself envying the scrawny shepherd. She wondered what Jessie's life had been like before the event. Had she had a girl or boy she adored? A family that loved and spoiled her? Did she still think of them? Miss them?

Pulling herself from her thoughts, she moved deeper into the woods. She carried her long gun with her in hopes of scaring up some fresh meat. Although she'd never had squirrel or rabbit, she would be more than happy to try either if she happened to stumble across one. Or even a bird such as a partridge. Beggars could not be picky, and at this point, with her ever-increasing hunger, she certainly felt the part of being a beggar.

Chapter Eight

"A gentleman is someone who does not what he wants to do, but what he should do."
- Haruki Murakami

Brian Pitman sat back silently watching as the woman and the dog roamed through the woods. The younger woman was still back at the camp they'd set up, dozing. He'd been trailing them for the past two days, wondering, watching, and waiting.

He knew he should skirt around them and move on his way, but part of him held back. He was staying behind them. Yesterday he'd thought the dog, the one the woman called Jessie, had spotted him. He'd been ready to put it down if necessary. Thankfully it hadn't come to that. He liked dogs. Better than most people actually. People had always let him down. Dogs didn't. They were known for their loyalty and devotion.

Sweating from the heat of the sun, he stripped off his coat revealing muscular arms covered in tattoos. He traced a finger over one of them and grimaced. Too many memories associated with these black and blue ink outlines. Memories that flashed and sizzled, choked and burned in the back of his mind.

An X with skull and dagger. He'd earned every single tattoo that adorned his shoulders, arms, and chest. To other prisoners, the tattoos represented power and respect and gave him high ranking status. To him, they represented pain, blood, and death.

How he ended up in Massachusetts was a long and sordid story, one he'd rehashed a thousand times in his mind. Prison had left him plenty of time for that. The long days and even longer nights as he paced back and forth in a 4-by-8 foot cell. He could still feel the cold bars as his hands clasped them in desperation, could still taste and smell the harsh, bitter, ammonia cleaner they had used on the one metal toilet and the cement floors as they cleaned. With a tug of anger, he pushed these memories away.

He had been born a southern boy from Tennessee. The North East was a cold and unforgiving place; he hated it.

The event, in his opinion, was a Godsend. It helped him get out of prison and be on his way home. Many people died those first few months, but he didn't care, just as no one cared when they locked him away. The taste of these memories was as bitter and as poisonous as the red apple the witch gave to Snow White.

No police or correctional officers were chasing him, hell; most were either dead or worried about their own lives and families to be bothered with him. So, with a light step and home on his mind, he headed out, sticking to back roads and wooded trails and avoiding the small towns and larger cities, thus avoiding conflict.

In prison, he'd been the toughest dog on the cell block, not too many messed with him as they knew his reputation and feared him. Out here, though, it was a different story. He knew there were badasses roaming the streets much worse than he'd seen in prison.

Keeping his eyes on the woman and dog, he pulled a tin of chew from his pocket and stuffed a pinch in his cheek. Bitter, acrid saliva filled his mouth, and he spat onto the ground. He hated the chew but craved it. Checking the tin, he saw that there was only a pinch or two left. Oh well, the withdrawals would be a bitch but nothing he couldn't handle.

As he looked down at the scars on his arms and hands he realized, the one thing prison had taught him was just how much he could handle, and he found, much to his pain and suffering, he could handle a lot.

He watched as the woman dug up plants, and it piqued his curiosity. She was smart; he'd give her that. Fiddleheads, dandelions, and tiny purple violets. All edible. She carried a long gun across her shoulders. He smiled as he wondered how good of a shot she was. It was a big gun for such a small woman. At best guess he thought her to be 5′2 at the most. She carried a Sako 75 if he wasn't mistaken.

Smiling, he watched as she pulled the rifle, which was slung across her back, and raised it to her shoulder. She had a bead on a gray squirrel. Shaking his head, he waited for the boom and laughed softly. That gun would decimate a critter that small. Hell, there'd be nothing left of it. She'd be better off throwing rocks at the damn thing if she wanted it for food, which he suspected she did — getting up from his crouched position cringing as his knees popped loudly, he slowly made his way back to where he set up his camp.

His stomach rumbled noisily as he dug through his pack for a piece of jerky. He too could use some fresh food. Slinging his rifle across his shoulder, he made his way toward the ridgeline and away from the women and their dog. They'd likely hear his shots, but he would put enough distance between himself and them that they would not know from which direction the noise was coming, but it would also serve to scare them.

He noticed in following them the past few days how oblivious they were danger around them. This, at once, infuriated him. They acted as though they were alone in these woods, a big mistake on their part that could get them hurt or killed. Not that he cared what happened to them, but then again, he didn't particularly want to see harm come to them either.

These were dangerous times, and there were others out there in the woods that were far more dangerous than him. He wasn't the only one that had escaped from that prison he'd been confined to. And those others that raced out of there alongside him? Well, some of them were some pretty twisted and nasty animals.

Hiking upward, he let his mind drift. He thought about the two women and the dog. Mother and daughter? Sisters? The one woman looked old enough to be the younger girl's mother. He thought of his mother, and a tug hit his heart. Cringing, he curled his hands into fists as guilt sang through his veins. He hadn't seen her in more than ten years. Ten years of a life sentence.

His parents were getting up there in age. The trips from Tennessee to Massachusetts were infrequent and hard on them. He wondered if the virus had taken them. Or if not the virus, then something else. At this thought, his eyes filled with tears, and with a shaking hand, he brushed them away. He couldn't imagine what they'd been through because of him. He should have been there with them.

Both his parents were pretty tough mountain people. His father was an expert marksman with a gun, a tough bastard in his own right — tough, boy how he'd known that growing up. To say his father was not the kindest of people would be putting it lightly. His dad was a bastard. Always had been, but he'd also taught Brian to be tough and resilient. He'd taught him many skills, how to do a hard day's work, how to hunt, fish and fight. Yeah, the old man taught him a lot.

His mom, on the other hand, was a kind, gentle, and tender woman, much to his father's dismay. He'd been tough on her too, but she had the strength and determination it took to put up with him.

Their family homestead was completely self-sufficient — one hundred acres of wild land. Tall hardwood trees forested the property and surrounded wide open fields. They all worked that land till their hands bled, but he'd learned early on in life not to complain. Home, he just wanted to get home. To see his mom and yes, even the bastard that was his father.

The yearling doe stood in the shadow of the ridgeline. Beautiful and majestic. He concentrated on quieting his breath. Pulling the rifle up to his shoulder, he looked through the scope and picked his spot then aimed and fired, bringing her down quickly. As he stood over her body, he bent his head and sent up a silent prayer of thanks. Not out of reverence for the doe's life, but rather out of a lifelong habit ingrained in him at a very young age.

He'd get about sixty pounds of meat from the animal. Much of that, he would dry and pack for later meals. But tonight, he would fill himself with fresh meat. His stomach growled as he set about skinning and harvesting the meat, letting the doe's warm blood run over his hands as he worked expertly with his knife.

Although he concentrated on the task before him, he was also astutely aware of his surroundings. His thoughts once again drifted to the women and the dog. They were hungry too. Desperately hungry, he thought. He could slip some fresh meat into their campsite after dark after they turned in for the night — something to help them out.

But doing so would alert them to his presence in the area. Was it worth the risk? And why should he even care? It wasn't like they were anything to him. Growling, he shook his head. It angered him that he thought to even bother with them. Those women were not his problem, and he'd be damned if he would make it so.

It took him less than an hour to skin, clean and pack up the meat from the small doe. The remains he left for the scavengers. They'd make quick work of it. He hiked back down to his camp just before the sun sank below the horizon.

He slung his pack onto the ground and stretched the ache from his shoulders. He built a small fire, spit some choice cubes of deer meat onto a green stick, and once the fire burnt down, he set the spits onto the coals and let the meat cook slowly. His eyes roamed the woods, and his ears listened for any sound of predators that he knew smelled the aroma of cooking meat.

While he waited, he took out his knife, grabbed the sharpening stone from his hiking pack, and rubbed it steadily and slowly across the blade. A sharp knife was, to him, one of the most valuable tools he owned.

He was good with a knife, actually very good with a knife. He let his mind drift as the stone, and his hand worked as one. The hiss of the knife blade as it ran across the stone was music to his ears. It was a comforting and familiar sound.

He would bring meat to the women. He couldn't let them be hungry. He thought of his sister, Talia. She'd been hungry once. Near starvation actually. His stomach curled in anger as he thought of her, and his breath caught in the back of his throat as a dark grimace touched his lips. She had once been an innocent, happy young girl.

When he found her, that girl no longer existed. In her place was a fearful, emaciated, traumatized, and pitiful shadow. They had ruined her. They had destroyed her. And he had destroyed them. And it hadn't been pretty or easy or merciful. It had been bloody and slow as he tortured every breath from their bodies; yet it had satisfied him in an unexplainable way. At a gut level. The screams and cries as they pleaded for their lives. The same way his sister had pleaded with them.

Then he did it again and again, to all those that followed; too many for him to count. But each one had been a masterpiece. And each one caused him no regret — not one ounce of pity for those he had sent to hell. Because of his sister, his heart had turned to cold stone. And he had shown not one iota of mercy to those responsible.

Yes, he would bring the women some meat. He wouldn't let them feel the hunger that Talia had felt.

Chapter Nine

Beth woke just as the sky had turned from an inky black to a wispy gray. She rubbed her eyes with her fists, itching away the grit and grime. Crawling from the tent, she stretched and yawned. Her body protested with twinges of pain, and she worked the stiffness from her joints.

Yesterday's rest day had done both her and Sarah good, and although they ate of fresh greens and noodles, they hadn't had any protein. That would soon become a problem for them if she didn't find a way to get them some meat.

Shrugging away the worry, she made her way to the cold fire pit. A warm fire would take away the morning chill and also heat water for coffee. She thought of the real coffee she'd had at Jim's farm and sighed. God how she wished for real coffee. The dark, smooth taste of it. The coffee she would soon be drinking was not real. Instant. Bitter tasting and weak. But it was better than none at all.

As she broke twigs to start the campfire, her eye caught on a bundle sitting on a rock nearby of what looked to be bloodied rags. Curious and hesitant, she approached the rock. A chill tickled its icy fingers down her spine.

Bloody rags? Where had they come from? Had Sarah hurt herself during the night and not wake her? Walking closer to it, she bent over for a closer look. Picking up a stick, she lifted one corner of the rag to find two large hunks of meat.

"What in the hell?"

Confusion, disbelief, and fear ran like an electric current through her chest.

"Meat? Where did this come from?"

She was still muttering to herself when Sarah quietly moved up behind her, scaring her half to death and she stifled a scream. She hadn't heard her come out of the tent. Turning, she looked at her with a scowl.

"Sarah? Did you hear anyone in our campsite last night?"

Sarah shook her head, and Beth grimaced.

"Shit!"

Someone had brought them meat. That meant someone had seen her hunting yesterday; someone had been watching her as she picked the plants. The thought of this made her heart thud fearfully, and her breath stop. She'd been careless, once again. Jessie, by her side, whined as if she sensed her nervousness, and she reached down and softly stroked the dogs head.

She murmured, "It's okay, girl. I didn't hear anyone either."

Turning to Sarah, she smiled, trying to hide her fear. "Okay, well I guess we'll be having fresh meat for breakfast then hustling our butts out of here."

She picked the bloody package up off of the rock and carried it to the fire pit. Her gun, the handgun she wore on her side, was still in the tent and she asked Sarah to get it for her. She also instructed Sarah to grab her own as well.

"We both need to be locked and loaded, Baby Girl," she whispered as she began to cook the meat. A trembling smile touched her lips as she saw Sarah nod solemnly in response. She didn't want the young girl to know how terrified she was.

The meat sizzled and popped over the fire and her mouth watered as she waited. The aroma sent her belly into a chorus of growls. Sarah, crouching beside her, eyed the meat hungrily.

"Almost done, Baby Girl," Beth said softly.

After breakfast they broke camp and hiked hard and steady, only stopping for a few brief minutes every few hours for a quick drink. She pushed both Sarah and Jessie forward with quick, sharp words. She was nervously alert and jumping at every little noise in the woods along either side of the trail. Worry gnawed at her stomach. Whoever had left them the gift of the meat that morning was following them... or near them... or watching them. Her hand stayed resting on the butt of her gun, and her fingers teased the cool, smooth wood. How could she have not heard anyone entering their camp last night? How had Jessie not heard anyone entering? She felt her face flush with guilt and shame. She had to do better to keep herself and Sarah safe.

Shaking her head in frustration, she pushed herself harder as she wound her way up a steep and rocky hill. She muttered out loud every few feet, drawing curious glances from Sarah.

"Keep your head on a swivel, push hard, put the miles between you and them. Keep your eye out for cover. Run if you have to." All great advice from the authors. Dorene Stalter's voice rang softly in her mind.

"Don't panic. Just keep moving."

The meal of meat had given both her and Sarah full stomachs; something neither of them had had in many weeks. Even Jessie got her fill of food for a change and responded to this by bouncing happily along the trail in front of them.

Sweat rolled in ticklish rivulets down her back, soaking her light tee shirt, causing it to stick uncomfortably to her skin. She swiped at a sheen of sweat on her forehead and cursed under her breath as she fought for each step.

Her breath came in little gasps, and her chest burned as the hill in front of her became steeper and steeper. From behind her, she could hear Sarah struggling as well. Grabbing onto a spindly tree, she bent to catch her breath and hissed.

"Shit! I need to take a minute."

Sarah slumped onto the ground beside her, gasping lightly and mopping her sweaty brow with the back of her hand.

"Only a few more miles and we should be getting close to the Wilbur Clearing Shelter. We'll find a spot to camp near that."

She felt bad for pushing so hard.

Sarah nodded tiredly.

According to the AT Trail map Beth carried, once they reached the shelter, they would have done an average of eight and a half miles. It wasn't bad for a day's hike but not as many miles as she'd hoped to reach either. It pissed her off that they were moving so slowly.

Although their bodies were conditioning to the terrain and stress of hiking, she had to remember; she wasn't a spring chicken anymore either. At forty-eight years old, she had some miles on this machine she called her body. And a lot of those miles were hard earned. And Sarah, poor Sarah had come to her already underweight, struggling with beat up and blistered feet and traumatized by what life had handed her.

Couple that with the poor diet of mainly carbohydrates, low caloric intake and lack of fresh vegetables and protein it was a wonder that either of them was able to keep up the pace she'd set, never mind hike the terrain they had. A pang of guilt nagged at her as she thought of how hard she was pushing Sarah.

They arrived at the shelter at dusk. Although it would have been nice to stay there for the night, surrounded by three walls and a roof, she pushed deeper off the trail and into the woods. The shelter lay on the main trail and in her opinion, it would leave them too exposed should anyone come along.

In another time she would have easily camped there and enjoyed the company of other hikers. She would have sat by the campfire, chatted with other hikers, perhaps shared a beer. But, not now. Not since the event. Since the event, she purposely avoided people and with good reason. Everything changed; life changed. The body she'd left lying on her kitchen floor all those weeks ago had been proof of that. She'd trusted her neighbor. And that trust had damn near cost her life.

Chapter Ten

Brian pushed himself further and further up the trail; pausing from time to time to listen carefully to the woods around him. Yesterday while hunting, he'd heard human activity near where he'd propped himself against a tree to rest. After skinning and cleaning the doe he'd shot, he sat silently watching curiously a group of three men moving through the thick woods a mere several hundred yards from his location.

It appeared they were hunters. They all carried rifles and packs. He listened as they talked quietly and picked up a few fragmented sentences. From the looks of them, he determined they were just good old boys looking to feed themselves. Not anything to worry about, but it was still too close for comfort. Just in case, he'd slept lightly and on alert back at camp that night.

He wanted no surprises nor anyone stumbling into his camp by accident. He kept his gun within reach, by his side, his knife sharpened, and at the ready.

His mind wandered to the women. When he'd visited their campsite in the darkness of early dawn, they hadn't heard him. The damn dog hadn't even heard him. He scowled at the thought of it.

"That was dangerous." He muttered.

He purposefully even made a little noise to alert them when leaving, yet none of them even stirred.

Shaking his head, he growled softly under his breath and rolled over. "They're sitting ducks. Careless."

He didn't care. What were they to him other than strangers, a nuisance? He tried to tell himself he didn't care but couldn't escape the question.

Unable to sleep, he made a sweep of the area, patrolling within listening distance to where they were. His mind raced while he moved from tree to rock to tree, checking the woods for danger. Why was he purposely staying behind them anyway? He could've passed by them many times, left them in the dust. He was a stronger and faster hiker and yet here he was, behind them, trailing them like a guard dog trails its master. His behavior confused him. He'd always been a loner, always had a don't give a shit attitude.

Disgusted, he kicked angrily at a stone in his path, sending a jolt of pain singing through his foot.

His old man had taught him to be hard and cold. To look out for number one. And he remembered the words so often said to him.

"Look out for number one. Don't get

involved."

That sentiment had served him well for most of his life. So why now? Why these two women? Why did he feel that he was responsible for their safety? It shouldn't be his problem. He scoffed and turned back to his own site, mumbling to himself. "If they run into trouble because of their carelessness, then so be it. Look out for number one… take care of numero uno. I don't need or want any extra baggage."

His father's voice whispered in the back of his mind. "You've always been a chump boy. A sucker for a pretty face. Once a sucker, always a sucker," Brian shook his head and grimaced angrily.

"Fuck you, asshole," he muttered softly.

Thoughts of his father reminded him of Talia. It seemed that family was on his mind a lot lately. His old man was an asshole to him, but to Talia, he was doting and always gentle. She had been a daddy's girl, for sure. He wondered if the old man blamed himself for what happened to her.

Brian had been on a two-year tour in Afghanistan and was recently returned to the states. He was stationed at Fort Bragg when the call came in. Talia had been at the shopping mall with a group of friends and wandered off from the group to go the restroom. It was then that she just up and disappeared.

At first, the police thought she'd just run

away, but Brian knew better. There was no reason for her to run away. Only a couple of days later, a couple walking their dog found her purse and her cell phone on an old back road ten miles outside of town.

After an agonizing three-day search of the surrounding woods, they realized that she'd been kidnapped. Brian became the man he was today — a hunter, a killer.

It took him two years to find his sister. And in his search, he'd left a trail of bloodied corpses in his wake. The girl he'd brought home to his parents was not the same girl who had disappeared. Five months after she returned home, she committed suicide. Even thinking of it now brought him anguish — a wound re-opened and raw. One that seared his heart with a pain so deep that it would never go away. His baby sister had been gentle and sweet; her smile enough to soothe the even the worst of his temper. God, how he missed her.

The women were a half a mile ahead of him when he climbed a steep hill and spied them winding their way through a ravine below. His heart thudded in fear as he saw, not five hundred yards ahead of the women, coming from the opposite direction, a group of others on horseback. He counted three, and the women would be walking right into them.

"Shit!" he muttered as he picked up his pace, half running, half stumbling in his haste.

Looking up at the fading light, he knew nightfall would soon be on them.

It took him fifteen or so minutes to close the distance between himself and the women. But that fifteen minutes was almost too long. He worried he would be too late to help them.

∞

Beth cried out as the chubby fingers, wadded into a fist, slammed into her face. It sent jolts of broken pain soaring through her nose as if a nest of hornets had been let loose inside her head. She fell to the ground, dirt and pine needles filling her mouth as she landed on her face. She heard laughter behind her then screamed in agony as a swift kick landed on her left side. Retching and gagging, she fought to crawl away, her hands scrabbling at the dirt as she pulled herself forward.

Grit clogged her throat, and panic took her breath away. She tensed as she felt a hand from behind grab a fistful of her hair and roughly yank her to her feet. Turning, she clawed at the man's face, feeling her fingernails dig into his flesh, sticky with blood and skin. Another blow knocked the wind from her, and she struggled to breathe. A sob choked her, and she raised her head, looking for Sarah through swollen, tear-filled eyes. She spied her struggling with a man across the campsite.

Anger sizzled in her gut as she assessed the situation, she exploded up off of the ground only to be hammered once again by strong and punishing fists. A voice deep in her mind screamed that she had to keep fighting or these men would kill both her and Sarah. Sucking in a deep breath, she tasted her blood as it ran down the back of her throat, thick and choking. With a weak effort, she pushed herself up off the ground one more time and launched herself at her attacker, wrapping her bruised and bloodied hands into his hair as she screamed with fury. She became nothing but fists and fingernails, teeth, punches, and kicks, as she fought for her life.

Stars danced before her eyes as she fell to the ground, blinded by the blow to her head. Crawling, dragging sand and dirt that ground into her skin felt like the cuts of a thousand tiny shards of glass as her breath rasped through bloodied teeth. She sank weakly into the darkness that danced at the edge of her vision.

∞

He heard the scream just as he rounded the bend in the trail. Dropping behind a cluster of tangled brush, he saw one of the women, the older one, fall to the ground and bounce back up like a jack in the box toy. In her hand, she held a big rock and swung it toward a man's head. He heard the thud of it meeting flesh.

The man, large and round, struck out with a meaty fist and punched her again, spinning her on her feet like a puppet. He heard laughter as another man held the struggling younger woman in a bear hug while she kicked and clawed at him.

The third man stood off to the left of him leaning against a tree with a grin on his face, holding the reins of the horses. The older woman's face bled profusely from the repeated punches she was taking, yet she fought back like a hellcat. Each time she fell, she'd pop back up swinging, and this brought a chorus of laughter from all of the men in the group. Brian urged her silently to stay down. He needed her to stay down!

Pulling up his rifle, sucking in a deep breath, he drew a bead on the man leaning against the tree. Sliding his finger to the trigger, aiming center mass, he tapped it lightly. The man slid to the ground, startling the horses who broke free and bolted for the woods.

Before the other two men could respond, a growl and snarl erupted from behind the trees somewhere off to his right. He watched as the dog exploded into the fray, launching itself in a black and white fury, onto the man holding the younger woman.

The older woman, he saw, was now crawling on the ground, too beaten to get up as her attacker stood over her. He had a hand full of her long hair and was trying to drag her back to him.

Brian saw her leg strike out behind her,

connecting with the man's shin. And the man, screamed out a howl of pain and anger as he pulled her to her feet by a fistful of her hair and crushed her up against him, holding her in front of him as a human shield. Brian swore under his breath. He couldn't take the shot in fear of hitting her. Snarls and shouts, screams, and cries filled his ears.

Standing up, he sucked in a deep breath and pulled the knife from its leather sheath on his belt. He couldn't take the chance of hitting the woman. Bloodlust, anger, cold and dead mindlessness filled him as he stormed toward the man. He became the animal. And the animal in him needed to taste blood.

"You just made your biggest mistake!" he growled through clenched teeth as he launched himself at the man, knocking the woman out of the way with one push.

The bullet hit him before he'd even heard the explosion from the gun, but not before he sank his knife up to its hilt into the other man's chest. Pain radiated from his left thigh like a kick from a thousand-pound mule, and he sank to the ground as he heard an explosion of shots from his left.

Craning his neck, he saw the beaten and bloodied woman up on her knees, gun in her hand and a bloody grimace on her mouth as she pulled the trigger several more times. Darkness seeped into the edge of his vision. The next thing he felt was soft hands on his face and heard a faraway voice, shaky and soft, whisper in his ear.

"Don't worry mister; I got ya."

Chapter Eleven

Beth clamped her teeth onto her lower lip, willing herself to stop shaking as tears poured down her face. It all happened so fast. One minute she and Sarah were walking along, looking for a spot to set up camp and the next, they were attacked.

She didn't hear them coming. And by the time she realized what was happening, it was too late to run. Now there were three bodies on the ground, two dead, one near dead. And then there was the man who had appeared from out of the woods, shooting and swinging, fighting to save them.

Hearing a moan, she got up from where she knelt. Her head spun dizzily with the sudden movement. Her breath rasped through her nose, which she was sure was broken. Her eyes felt nearly swollen shut, and her face felt as though she'd just encountered a battering ram as pain rocked her teeth. She sucked up a mouthful of blood and spat it onto the ground. Her jaw clamped tight, fighting the pain as she moved slowly, hissing with every breath.

Pausing, she sucked in a deep breath and watched through swollen eyes as Sarah crawled on her hands and knees toward her. Reaching out, she folded the girl into her arms.

"It's okay; we're okay," she crooned softly as the girl shook with dry, soundless sobs. She felt Sarah's gentle hands stroking her face, each light touch sending new jolts of pain through her.

Gazing across the top of her head, she looked at the barely conscious man that Jessie stood guard over. She'd taken two shots at him; one missed completely, but the other had gutted him. He wasn't going to die easy — gutshot and writhing in pain.

She untangled Sarah from her arms and with a wince, walked over to where the man lay in a pool of blood. Kneeling, she looked straight into his eyes.

"You're gonna pay for this, bitch!" he spat between gurgling gasps. She said nothing as she stared blankly at him.

"Bobby is gonna make you wish you were dead by the time he's through with you," the man hissed.

Shaking her head, she pulled the knife from her side and with one swift motion, slit his throat. She watched in fascination as his eyes widened in horror as the breath struggled out of his body. She'd be damned if she'd waste another bullet on this sorry soul.

Standing stiffly, she turned and walked back over to where Sarah stood looking down on the stranger that had saved them. Kneeling, her body screaming in agony as waves of pain crashed through her. She checked out his wound. A clean shot through his upper thigh, outer edge. She motioned for Sarah to help her.

Together they turned the man over onto his side where she saw the gaping exit hole. The bullet had gone neatly through. Sighing, she nodded and whispered shakily to Sarah.

"Okay, I can deal with this."

It was pitch black by the time she cleaned, stitched, and bandaged the man's wound. Sarah had been busy: she set up the tent, scoured the woods for the man's pack and rifle and gathered twigs and sticks for a fire. She then scavenged from the bodies, taking anything that would benefit them.

Beth, exhausted and spent, sat on the ground by the fire and rested. Water heated in a pot over the flames and Beth watched in miserable pain as Sarah took a tee shirt from one of the men, ripped it into strips and dipped the rags into the water. She then gently ministered to Beth's wounds. Her touch was so soft and tender that Beth couldn't help but let the tears flow down her face. Sarah made a soft mewling shhhhing sound as she hugged her tightly. They sat this way for several moments, Beth drawing comfort and strength from Sarah.

The night closed in around them as the fire soothed their tired minds, casting shadows that danced among the trees. Dozing lightly,

Beth was surprised when Sarah sat down by the campfire with a western guitar she'd taken from one of the men and began strumming it lightly. After a few minutes of strumming, she sank into a Leonard Cohen song that brought tears to Beth's eyes. Hallelujah.

As she listened, memories flooded her heart and her mind. Memories that almost broke her. She looked at Sarah in amazement. A girl who looked to be barely sixteen and had no voice was strumming the guitar like she'd been doing it all her young life. Her fingers teasing beauty from the strings stretched tight across the wood. Beauty in the ugliness of the day, beauty to wash the soul of freeing it from the pain that brought so much despair.

It took both of them to drag the unconscious man into the tent. He would wake soon enough. There was nothing more she could do other than wait. Fixing a small meal, they ate in worried silence. Jessie lay quietly at their feet, waiting for the few nibbles she knew would be coming. Her mind churned with questions.

Who was this, Bobby? The one the dead man said would come looking for her? A brother? A friend? Whoever he was, she knew that he would probably come looking for the man she'd killed, and she hoped by the time this Bobby found this mess; they would miles away. But the problem was, she couldn't leave the injured man in her tent behind.

Silently she prayed he would wake up soon. He had risked his life helping them; and she would stand by him until he was ready to travel. Time was of the essence. She didn't want to be anywhere near here if the man called Bobby did come looking. Looking across the fire at Sarah, she nodded tiredly.

"Well, girl. We got a problem."

Sarah's ice blue eyes lifted to hers.

"We might have some bad men coming our way. We can't run and leave the man behind. We're gonna have to stay put until he wakes up. So that leaves us with having to stand guard all night. I'll take the first watch."

Sarah nodded in response and then smiled tightly as she stood up. Beth thought she was going into the tent to get some sleep and was surprised as the girl picked up a stick of wood from the fire and using it as a torch, walked off toward the dark woods. Curious, she jumped up, wincing in pain as her body protested the sudden movement. She turned on her headlamp and followed her.

"What are you doing?"

Sarah turned and motioned with her hand, then began to dig a hole with a stick. Confused, she watched as Sarah dug several more circling the campsite, about twenty in all. Shaking her head, she wondered what in the hell the girl was up to. Sarah then began collecting solid sticks from the woods by the firelight from her torch.

Carrying them back to the campfire, she grabbed Beth's knife from her pack on the ground and began whittling to create sharpened ends on each stick. When she had a pile of several dozen or so, she carried them to the dug holes and stuck them deep into the dirt and covered them over with leaves and brush. Beth laughed as she watched the young girl busily creating a series of ankle breaking, foot puncturing booby traps.

"Where in the hell did you learn to do that?" she teased. Sarah cut her eyes toward Beth and smiled coldly.

"I guess I'll never know but dang girl! Great job!"

It took them several hours to lay booby traps outside of their camp. Beth, sore, moved slowly. Not only did Sarah create ankle breaking, foot puncturing hellish holes, she also created wooden spears, driven at an angle deep into the ground, which if walked into in the dark would surely pierce and puncture the skin. It was hard and sweaty work, but they both felt a little safer having it done.

Chapter Twelve

"In moments of pain, we seek revenge." -Ami Ayalon

Bobby Belanger watched as the sun sank low on the horizon. Scowling, he threw his cigarette onto the ground and stomped a sneakered foot down on it. Billy, Tim, and Elroy should have been back by now, and he was getting a bit worried. He worried they had run into problems over the border in Connecticut. That was Compound territory. A thorn in his side. Whenever he'd sent his men on a run up that way, they ran into the compound militia. A group of men armed to the teeth and determined to keep him from raiding the towns adjacent to them.

Tamara moved up beside him and wrapped an arm around his waist. He pushed her away angrily, knocking her to the ground. He paid little attention to the glare of hatred she shot at him. She mattered little to him. She was just his whore, and as soon as he tired of her, he'd replace her with some fresh meat.

But for now, she was a place to plant himself when the need arose. Other than that, she was an inanimate object, in his opinion. Looking down at her, his mouth twisted into a cold grin.

The guys had been on a mission. They needed more women for barter and they needed the special package that was waiting for him. So he'd sent them to a neighboring town to snatch and grab. He had twenty women he now pimped out. He needed at least ten more as the demand was high. They should have been there and back hours ago. He wondered if they ran into trouble. He knew he should have sent Harris and Kevin along with them. Shit! Well, it was too late now to go looking. But if they weren't back at the crack of dawn, he'd gather up the boys and go and find them.

He didn't give a shit about Tim and Elroy, but Billy was his baby brother. He'd never forgive himself if something happened to that punk. An uneasy, unsettled feeling sank into the pit of his stomach, and his lips curled into a grimace.

Life had been good for him since the Event. He had all the booze and guns he could ever want; drugs, food, and women. He saw the writing on the wall and taken advantage quickly after the breakdown of law.

He'd gathered up his good buddies, and they quickly became the law of the land in his town. It was his idea to start building their enterprise with pimping out the women, and he found plenty of men that were happy to pay any price for the opportunity to fulfill their twisted and often sadistic needs.

His women came in all shapes, sizes, and ages. Some of his clients liked them young and fresh; some liked them a bit older and more experienced. It didn't matter to him; he met their demands with a variety of supply.

Lighting a cigarette, he drew a deep drag and coughed it out. He glanced down at Tamara. She had a few more go's in her, and he motioned for her to follow him. Obediently she got up from the ground, and with her head hung low, followed him into the house. In her heart, she knew he would one day very soon kill her. But she vowed she would get him first. This thought brought a smile to her bruised and battered face. Bobby liked to use his fists on her. And he used them often.

Society since the Event became like the wild west and Bobby thrived in this environment. He thought of himself as a modern day, Billy the Kid. People reverted to the savagery of those days. Men and guns, fists and bloodletting. Taking what they wanted or needed from those who couldn't defend themselves.

Yes, this was his time. Before the event, he'd always walked that fine line between jail and freedom. People who didn't give him the time of day, who looked at him like he was some slithering, slimy thing that just crawled from beneath a rock, now feared him.

Now they called him boss or sir. And the

women who'd pointed their noses high in the air, who cast him looks of disdain and revulsion, now catered to him. His father was the first man he'd killed after the event. That fat and slovenly bastard deserved every bit of pain and punishment Bobby gave him. And he'd given him plenty. What that man did to Billy and him? Welp, let's say, he got what was coming to him.

And his mama, she was just as bad. She screamed and cried as Bobby took down the old man. Her cries stopped when Billy shot her between the eyes, and the brothers both laughed hysterically as her body slunk to the ground like someone just let the air out of her obese tires. Drunks, both of them. Nothing but nasty and mean drunks. Yup, this was his time now.

He was a man of importance, gaining notoriety by the day as he networked outward. He walked into his office, a small alcove off of the living room, and shuffled maps and other papers from his desk. He pointed to Tamara and she obediently knelt on the floor next to his chair. He petted her on the top of her head, like he would a faithful and obedient dog, then laughed as he thought of this. That was it! She was his dog, and every dog deserved a pretty collar. He made a mental note to find one later and strap it around her neck. He'd find a leash too. This way, he could proudly parade her up and down the street for all his men to see.

On the wall behind him was a map of the

Northeast with red tacks placed in strategic places indicating towns and gang affiliations.

While others holed up through the winter in their homes, trying to outlast the virus and too afraid to venture out, he was busy building his presence to what it was today.

He started out in a small circle, covering towns that were nearby, within riding distance. Then as his gang grew, they traveled further and further. Much like a snowball rolling downhill, he gathered more resources and more fighting force.

He gazed at the map on the wall and smiled as he slid his hand roughly down the front of Tamara's shirt. He felt her tense beneath his touch, and he slapped her roughly.

"You are my property," he growled. He grinned in satisfaction as she nodded her head.

Out of Boston, Massachusetts, he networked with the Winter Hill Gang, a gang of its own notoriety, having been the home of the famous James Whitey Bulger. With his death, the gang underwent a shift in power but hadn't lost its prominent position. They now ran the entire South End Corridor.

From there he networked out to New York and hit the jackpot as he gained partnership with the Crips and the Folk Nation; both strong in numbers and resources. Through many tense meetings, give and take from all of the gang leaders, they took on the new foundation of merging into one group. The Tristate Alliance. They had become an army.

He thought of the first hectic and sketchy months of the event and how quickly these gangs had all taken control of their areas. This thought brought a grin to his lips. He had the wherewithal to move fast and hard; giving orders to take down the small town cops, gathering up the citizens one by one. As they moved from house to house, they took every available resource: food, guns, ammunition, medical supplies, and of course, the women that made up the foundation of his thriving business. The men had a choice, join him, or die. Most chose to join him.

Now through this hard and sometimes bloody work, he was sitting atop his own empire. Goods flowed in and out, trading for things they needed. He felt like a king, and this feeling led him to his next move.

He wanted the compound over the border in Connecticut. From recon trips he'd sent his men on, he knew the compound had a boon of resources. He also knew it was heavily defended. Wrinkling his brow, he thought of what he'd learned about the group.

The fighting force, led by a man named Roger, was dozens of men strong. His men ran into this force when raiding towns close to the Compound and the battles between them were bloody. He'd lost several men to those assholes.

Since then, he'd been slowly devising a plan of attack. They, the compound, stood in his way. In the way of him taking the whole of the Northeast in his ever-widening territory.

A knock on the door interrupted his thoughts. Harris entered and sat down on a chair opposite him. He shot a curious look at Tamara kneeling on the floor but said nothing.

"The boys are coming in from the south with fuel. It'll be here in three weeks."

Bobby nodded. Three weeks and they would have enough fuel to run the vehicles. That would be a game changer for him and his men.

"They have cleared the roads from New York to Boston. The tankers will be running right on time," Harris said.

The tankers he spoke of made their way across miles and miles of highway that were congested with abandoned vehicles. Time-consuming and difficult, the Crips from New York led the efforts in clearing the highways for easier networking between the major players. Bobby nodded.

"Good. How many women have we got for trade?"

"Right now, nineteen. We lost one last week to Ruben. She didn't make it," he sighed wearily. Ruben was a butcher. And twice now he'd unintentionally killed the women Bobby had pimped out to him.

"It's not enough. They want at least thirty," Harris replied. Bobby leaned back in the chair and rubbed his temples. Thirty meant another raid. And the death of another one of his whores, because of Ruben, meant that he was short on filling the demands of his clients. He would deal with Ruben later. But for now, he needed to strategize what town he would have to hit.

"Okay. Let me think about this. We need to plan another raid soon. Can't let our boys from the south down now, can we?" he chuckled.

Chapter Thirteen

This was the part of the business Bobby hated; the part that made him the most uneasy. He'd dealt with those formerly known as Crips many times, and although they were now part of the Alliance, he still had very little trust for them. They were a tricky and shady bunch of bastards, especially Thomias, the Alliance region leader. The way the man's eyes were always watching, shifting, and darting gave Bobby the impression that he was looking for any weakness he could use against him.

He had every right to be nervous. Thomias had a reputation for brutality, and Bobby thought the man would drive a knife into his own mothers back if he thought he would gain from it.

But necessity demanded that he deal with Thomias and his men. They desperately needed the fuel that this group was bringing to them. Fuel meant they could run their vehicles, expanding their raids further out, which in turn gained them more resources.

For the short raids, the horses were adequate. With the vehicles, he could hit harder and faster. It was a win-win all the way around. It pissed him off having to depend on others for what he needed though. He was never one to play along well to the group think mentality. But, small towns didn't carry the large amounts of fuel he needed to keep his small community going, so that made him have to play nice. This stuck in his craw as painfully as a thorn. He was king of his own castle so to speak and yet found, even as king, there were others he was forced to answer to.

Chapter Fourteen

Brian woke angrily. Pain radiated in hot waves from his hip to his knee, and he swung violently at the soft arms that pressed his shoulders down. With a start, he struggled against the darkness. His breath rasped angrily between his clenched teeth, and he let out a volley of profanity.

∞

Obscenities flying from within the tent sent Beth careening to her feet. Stumbling against the pain that assaulted her body; she clenched her teeth. She'd been dozing by the fire, drifting in and out as the night closed in around her. Awake enough to hear the chirping of the night creatures, awake enough to hear a branch snap.

She entered the dark tent with her headlamp switched on to see a nervous Sarah trying to restrain the injured man from getting up.

"Mister, it's okay. Be still; you're injured," she hissed as Sarah looked at her with wide and fearful eyes. The last thing she needed was for him to bust open the stitches she'd just put in a few hours earlier.

"Get this woman off of me!" the man

growled in response. She motioned for Sarah to back up a bit. She watched as the man struggled to a sitting position. Jessie stood at the doorway of the tent, growling softly.

"Call that mutt off!" Brian said angrily.

Beth reached out a calming hand to the dog.

"She won't hurt you. Your shouting scared her is all," she explained. The man glanced at her in irritation.

"How bad is my leg?" he asked.

"The bullet went clean through. A flesh wound. Don't be a baby," she snapped hotly "I cleaned the wound and stitched you up. It'll hurt like hell for a while, but I think it'll heal nicely."

He nodded. Yes, it was hurting like hell already, but he was thankful it wasn't worse.

"My name is Brian. Did you just call me a baby?" he snickered.

She smiled, then laughed.

"Yes, I did. I'm Beth, this is Sarah, and the dog is Jessie."

Brian nodded and then shifted his weight a bit to get more comfortable.

"Thank you for stitching me up."

She nodded. This man had saved her and Sarah's ass, and he was thanking her? She was the thankful one. If he hadn't come along, she couldn't imagine what those men would have done to them both. The thought sent a tingle down her spine. Yes, she could imagine but didn't even want to go there.

"Are you kidding me? Shit, thank you for saving our hides!" she replied. "Are you hungry? Thirsty?"

Brian nodded. He was both. He watched as Beth moved from the tent and then came back in carrying a bottle of water and a cup of what looked to be a noodle mixture. Uncapping the bottle, he took a long and deep drink. It felt good on his parched throat. Then with three large bites, he ate the noodle mixture. It was cold, but he didn't care. Food was food for a hungry belly.

She apologized for the small amount of food she'd given him, and he waved her off.

"It's fine. I wasn't that hungry," he lied. He looked at Sarah, who sat in the shadowed corner of the tent watching him. She hadn't said a word, not even when he was yelling at her and pushing at her as she tried to hold him down — not one syllable, not one grunt.

"Hi Sarah, I didn't hurt you, did I?" he asked. She shook her head. He cast a glance at Beth.

"She doesn't talk," she explained.

The night went from clear and starlit to overcast and rainy. Sitting in the tent, the four of them crowded together; Beth shared the last few pieces of beef jerky she had left. Sarah wolfed hers down in two huge bites while Beth nibbled at her own slowly, savoring every tough and dry bite, washing it down with water. The fire went out, and the woods were buzzing with activity from the night creatures around them.

"So," Beth muttered between bites, "I think the men that attacked us earlier has a friend or family member named Bobby. And he's gonna be pissed when he finds his men dead," she finished. Brian listened quietly and then shook his head. His leg ached.

"I think at first light we need to beat feet out'a here," he suggested.

He didn't know if the man Beth killed was blowing smoke or telling the truth and he wasn't about to stick around to find out. Those men were on that trail for a reason, and he suspected hunting was not their primary goal. He'd seen men like them before. Hard and mean with no consideration for anyone but themselves, and now that the law was not around to keep them in check? Well, it just made for a very bad situation all the way around.

Beth nodded in agreement. It was true. The faster they could leave, the better off they would be. But there was one problem.

"How are you going to hike over this terrain with an injured leg? You're injured, Brian! You need a few days to heal before you start putting too much stress on your leg."

"I will manage it. We can't stay here," he argued back.

Although she didn't know this man at all, the steely glare in his eyes told her that he would indeed push on.

"You're crazy. No, we stay," she replied stubbornly and shook her head. Brian turned his gaze up to her and swore in frustration.

"It is a wonder you haven't been killed yet! Or better yet, you haven't gotten her killed! "he said as he waved a hand at Sarah. "You skip along like your walking in a Sunday park, not paying attention to anything around you. You act as though you are oblivious to how dangerous this world has become!" he ground out angrily. "We can't stay! If what the dead man said is true, we are going to be hunted! I am not staying here to be a sitting duck! You stay if you want. I am leaving!"

She bit down hard on her lower lip as she felt tears sting the back of her eyes. This jack ass didn't know anything about her or what she'd gone through in the past week. He didn't know that she was doing the best she knew to do! She felt blind anger rushing through her as she struggled against the tears. Through clenched teeth and hitching sobs, she tore into him savagely.

"You don't know me! You don't know what I've been through! How dare you! I don't know how to do this! I don't know how to live like this! I am just trying to survive every single freakin moment of every day! I hate this new world! I hate that I am not as smart or a prepper or a fighter! I want to go home, but I have no home anymore. I am hungry and scared all of the time! My feet hurt, my face hurts from getting used as a punching bag! I never asked for this! I was married, I had a daughter, a good life and now it's all gone!"

It was all true - every anguished word she uttered. She was just a normal, forty-eight-year-old woman who had strength, determination, and stamina to stay alive. Before the event she lived a normal, sedentary life; occasionally hiking or camping, but otherwise, pretty boring.

She knew standard medicine and herbal medicine; she knew basic life-saving skills. She watched television and loved having every convenience available. Her food came from the grocery store, wrapped neatly in plastic or boxed neatly in boxes. She didn't can food and she didn't prep, she didn't have any fighting skills other than knowing how to take a beating and defending herself in whatever way she could. She couldn't hunt.

Shit! She could barely load the two guns she had, and the most she knew about them was to point and shoot. But in the life she'd led, she didn't have to know these things. Like most people, she lived easily, contentedly. She never expected life to take the turn it had and hand her a shit sandwich.

Brian watched as she curled in on herself, sobs wracking her body. He watched in stunned silence as Sarah crawled across the small tent and wrapped her tiny body around Beth's and as Jessie crawled to them both and shielded them with her body. He didn't know how to handle this. A crying woman? And her anger?

He had experience dealing with other prisoners, hard and seasoned criminals, not emotional women. He felt like he'd just kicked a kitten and it made him cringe inside. And he felt like shit, like something he'd peeled off the bottom of his shoe. Of course, she didn't know. Of course, she was working to survive. Weren't they all? He coughed softly.

"I'm sorry."

Beth looked up at him. Her face streaked with tears, purplish bruises around her swollen eyes.

"I'm doing the best I can right now," she whispered. Brian nodded.

"I know."

Four long, cold, rainy days. The mud stuck to their shoes. The rain soaked their clothes. Each night as they crawled into the tent to rest, their bodies chilled and shaking, Beth prayed for the sun to return. Prayed for a hot meal, even if it was only the cheesy noodles she was so sick of eating. Her rocket stove ran out of fuel. They struggled to try to get even the smallest of fires lit and finally resorted to just eating day in and day out the dried deer meat that was part of Brian's food stash.

She was concerned about Brian. The first

day on the trail, he limped along slowly but pushed them through the miles. He urged them to keep going until long after dark. That night he tossed and turned with pain. She'd given him Tylenol, but she was running low on those. He needed a good warming herbal tea, one that would combat the pain and boost his healing. But without fire, she couldn't even do that for him.

For three more days they pushed hard along the trail. And Beth saw that Brian was struggling; his limp became more pronounced with each step. His cheeks flushed with what she suspected was a fever, and he'd developed a deep, raspy cough. He wouldn't give in; he wouldn't let them slow down, he refused to stop. And then there was Sarah; she too was struggling.

Yesterday she noticed Sarah was starting to cough as well. They were both coming down sick, with a cold? With the flu? She didn't know, but whatever it was, she didn't like what she was seeing.

In the past week, she learned a lot about this man who'd saved their lives. She'd learned too that although he tried to paint himself a criminal, a tough guy, he wasn't as bad as he'd portrayed himself to be. He had a soft side. Not one he showed willingly, but she saw it. She saw it in the way he would sneak a bite of food to Jessie or pet her ears as she lay at his feet. She saw it in the way he always passed the water bottle for her and Sarah to drink before he took his sip. Or the way he made sure Sarah was tucked up tightly in the sleeping bag while he laid beside them both in the tent. Yes, the little ways were the telling nature of this man that was now part of their little group. He didn't talk much about his past, and she suspected that it was filled with violence and pain. The tattoos on his arms were familiar. She'd transported many a prisoner in the back of the ambulance to and from the hospitals in her old life. Though she didn't ask him about them, figuring he would tell her in his own time. Or maybe he never would, and that was okay too.

That evening, as they struggled to stay warm inside the tent, she talked to both of them about their situation. They needed to get off the trail. They needed to find a place that was warm and dry, where they could hole up for a few days and regain some strength. They needed warm meals.

She suggested they make their way into the next town they came to, find an abandoned house or barn, and take a day or two to just rest. Their backpacks were soaked through with the rain as well as their clothes and sleeping gear. They were exhausted from the miles they'd laid under their feet, and now they were starting to get sick.

"I don't know much about a lot of things,

but one thing I do know a lot about is the human body and illness. If we keep pushing the way we have been, we aren't going to have to worry about this so-called creep Bobby finding us; we'll be dead on the side of this damn trail from illness and exhaustion with the wild animals scavenging our bodies," she finished.

Brian nodded. What she said made sense. His chest felt like there was a hundred-pound weight sitting on it, his lungs burned with each breath and raspy cough, and he felt like he was trying to suck air through a straw. He was sick and getting sicker by the moment. And he'd too noticed Sarah starting to cough as well.

"You're right. As much as I hate to have to stop and hunker down, I know if we don't, then…." he finished, shrugging his shoulders.

"Good, then it's settled. Come morning we'll make our way into town," Beth replied.

In the past week, they covered roughly sixty miles. An average of fifteen miles a day over rough, muddy terrain. They were roughly thirty or so miles from the Connecticut border. The next closest town on the Appalachian Trail Guide Map to where they were would be Webster Massachusetts. So, Webster, it would be.

She remembered visiting there many years ago for some festival or another that Mitch was always dragging her to. It was a small city compared to Boston but large, and spread out enough that they should be able to find shelter without too much problem in the more rural locations. She didn't like the idea of going off trail but what other choice did they have? Neither Sarah nor Brian would heal in these cold and wet conditions.

Settling in for the night, she closed her eyes and sighed thankfully for the four hours of sleep she'd get before Brian would wake her to take over sentry duties. With the warmth of the sleeping bag around her, she let her mind drift and her breath even out as she listened to the chirping of crickets as they lulled her to sleep and the soft rain pattering on the canvas of the tent.

She woke to Sarah tossing and thrashing beside her, the girls young body shaking with silent sobs. She turned on her headlamp and looked up to see Brian standing in the doorway of the tent. She pulled Sarah into her arms and cradled her, soothing her with soft words. She felt Sarah's arms circle her waist and tighten with fear as shadows from the nightmare lingered like ghosts in her mind.

"It's okay. You are just having a nightmare baby." She looked over the top of Sarah's head at Brian.

"She's okay. Just nightmares," she said as Sarah curled into her. Once she got her back to sleep, she quietly made her way out to sit next to Brian.

"Is she okay now?"

"Yes. She's been through a lot. I don't know what, but whatever happened to her has left her terrified and traumatized. I don't know what her father or those men did to her, but I can only guess," she said softly. Brian's eyes hardened as anger gripped him. She was just a child. A child!

Chapter Fifteen

Bobby smiled then grimaced as he picked absently at a scab on his face, his fingernails digging in deeply and coming away smeared with blood. Acne was a constant, and he often picked at it; thus, deep scars and pockmarks blemished his face. His brother and other two men were still missing. His package, a very expensive package, was still missing along with the group of women they were supposed to be bringing back.

He didn't give a rat's ass about the men other than Billy, but the package and the women? Yeah, he gave a shit about that. It cost him two of his best women for the package. Equivalent to thousands of dollars if the dollar been worth anything anymore. Human trafficking had always been a lucrative business. There were those who would pay to play at any price. And he saw that quickly and took advantage of it.

His mama didn't raise any dummies. Strike while the iron is hot; she'd always told him in her more sober moments. And strike he did. He took women and girls from every surrounding town within miles and used them for trade. The package that the boys were carrying was considered white gold...cocaine. The best of the best. Of course, he would cut it down, add some of his crappy shit, and trade it for ten times what he'd paid. Yup, big business.

He knew he should've gone after the boys, but he figured the rain slowed them down. Now it was going on a week, and he knew something must've happened to them. Someone or something must've stopped them.

Glancing out at the dark and stormy sky, he shrugged his shoulders. He hated being wet and cold, but there were those who were hounding him for what was in the package, and he'd have no choice but to brave the weather and get what was his. Slinging a jacket over his shoulders, he opened the door.

It took him five minutes to walk over to Harris' house. Knocking lightly on the door, he waited. It was opened by a sultry redhead with green eyes. One of his women. A gift to his second in command. She glanced at him, then lowered her eyes. She knew it was a death sentence to show him any disrespect.

"Come in, sir."

Walking through the door, he tossed his rain jacket onto a nearby bench and lit a cigarette.

"Where's Harris?"

"He'll be down in a minute. He's getting dressed, sir." Bobby nodded and then grinned as he grabbed for the woman and pulled her roughly against him. She'd been his favorite. One of the first he'd taken. He regretted giving her to Harris. As her body leaned into his, he felt himself harden. If he had more time, well, he let that thought float away. He didn't have time. He remembered well her screams as he stood over her husband and unloaded his gun into him. Those screams intensified with what came later. Pulling her against him, he nuzzled his face into her hair. She didn't resist.

"Mmmmm…I miss you, Caitlin," he murmured as his hand slipped inside of her robe.

"Ummm…get your hands off my woman!" Harris said then laughed as he descended the stairs into the hallway. His voice was teasing, but the expression of anger that flashed in his eyes was telling.

Bobby looked at him over the top of Caitlin's head and grinned, giving her one last hard squeeze before he pushed her roughly away. He knew at any time he chose; he could have the woman back. Harris would not dare challenge him.

"We have business. Let's talk man," he said as he followed Harris into the living room. Caitlin slunk quietly and quickly away. She knew her place.

"The boys haven't come back yet. We need to get a few of the men together, saddle up the horses, and go find out what happened to them," Bobby said as he took a sip of the coffee Caitlin brought them. He let his eyes linger on her for a moment before turning back to Harris. Horses were the main mode of transportation since the event. Gas was at such a prime; he greedily hoarded what little he had for the generator that kept his beer cold and his lights on.

Harris nodded. Shit, he didn't want to go traipsing through the mountains to find them. But he also was smart enough not to say so. Bobby had a volatile temper and pissing him off would be a big mistake. They'd been friends since childhood; he'd seen what happened to those that dared cross Bobby. And since the event, the man had become even more unstable… if that was even possible.

"Okay, who do you want me to grab?"

"I'm thinking you and me, and grab Kevin and Payson. They're both strong fighters if we run into any trouble out there," Bobby replied.

Harris nodded. Yes, Kevin and Payson were both good men to bring along.

"Okay, I'll get the ball rolling. Meet back at your house say in an hour?"

Bobby grinned. "Yup, time to go hunting I think." With one last lingering glance at Caitlin, he turned and walked out the door. Yes, he'd have to do something with her when he got back. Harris be damned. If he didn't like it, oh

142

well.

Chapter Sixteen

Curt Macomber, Spike as his friends called him, planted one foot in front of the other as he sloshed his way through the mud. Those boys destroyed his life. Now it was time to pay up. He'd been days behind them all the way, and today he hoped to make up the miles and time.

He carried a long gun on his back and two short ones on either hip. He carried a knife on his belt, one in his boot and another inside under his jacket strapped to his chest. Hearing soft voices and heavy footsteps, he slid off the side of the trail and crouched behind a thick stand of scrabbly brush. Two women, a man, and a dog walked by him, oblivious to his presence. They were on the short trail that would lead them to Pinesly Hill Road, a short strip of blacktop just outside of town. He paid little attention to them. They were not his business right now. Right now, his business was finding the three men who'd come into his town, come into his house, and destroyed his life.

He was not the man he'd been a six months ago. Six months ago, before the event, he'd been a cop and a damn good one. He'd been an upstanding citizen, well liked and respected in his town. He'd been a father, a husband, a little league baseball coach. He'd been the leader of their church and ministry counselor. The event changed him. Life, hardship, death, and lawlessness had changed him. And today he became killer. He had nothing left to live for nor anyone left to care about. It was gone.

The three men had shown up in town. He'd paid little attention. He'd learned to mind his own business and mind his own family. He knew drugs were running in and out of the area. He knew there was human trafficking. All the things he would have stood against before the event. But there was no law anymore other than the law of survival.

So, he minded his own business even though he knew the trafficking of drugs and women were going on as well as other much worse things. Now karma it seemed came to pay him back for minding his own business thinking that if he did, no one would bother with him.

Things changed when those three men came to his house. Those three men raped and murdered his beloved Karen. Those three men murdered his four-year-old and seven-year-old sons because they could. He'd been gone, hunting for any wild game that he could find in the area. That was his mistake, leaving his family unprotected. But their mistake was in choosing his house to ransack; their mistake was choosing his family to kill. And he was now going to correct that mistake.

With each sloshing, muddy step, he felt his heart shatter over and over again until he thought the pain would kill him. His thoughts turned to Karen, his sweet, gentle wife. Her laughter, her tears, her fear echoed in his mind. An ache filled his heart as he longed to hold her again, just one more time. What those pigs did to her gutted him.

He thought of his boys, the way Trevor, his four-year-old, would crawl into his lap at the end of each day and rest his little blonde head on his chest and fall asleep. And Jake, his seven-year-old, wanting to be a grown up and helping with a life that had gone from easy and carefree to troubled and hard. Those men put a bullet into each of his boy's heads. And stealing the light of life from their eyes. Tears trickled down his face, and he angrily wiped them away with a shaking hand.

He buried the three of them together. Hours of mindless pain as he'd dug the grave. He wrapped them together in a white sheet smelling of bleach that Karen washed and line hung to dry. Wrapped the boy's little arms around their mother so they could spend their eternal rest hugging each other. That day he left his humanity at the grave.

Chapter Seventeen

Beth woke and winced as the stiffness threatened to lock her joints. She slowly pulled herself from the tangled sleeping bag. The air was moist and humid, and she sighed in relief as she saw the sun beating down on the tent. The rain, thank God, had finally passed. She smelled wood smoke and knew Brian managed to get a fire going finally. Sucking in a breath against the pain in her ribs, she dressed quickly as thoughts of a hot cup of herbal tea, lured her out into the morning. Fire meant cooking, fire meant making medicine for Brian and Sarah.

The air smelled thick with smoke from the fire and of Pine and sunshine, and she took a deep breath then winced once again as pain from her ribs fired through her. She was sure at least two of her ribs were broken from the kick her attacker launched into her side. Sarah, seeing her expression of pain, moved gently beside her and looked at her with concern.

"No worries kiddo. I'm fine," Beth lied. She smiled as Sarah reached out her hand and gently laid it against her cheek. Brian coughed, and both women turned toward him.

"I'm fine too," he said then chuckled.

Everything was wet, their tent, their sleeping bags, clothes, everything. Slowly she sat down on a log Brian placed near the fire. Pulling her backpack toward her, she ruffled through the pockets and pulled out a bag of herbal tea. Licorice root, cinnamon, Echinacea, elecampane and ginger, a cold and flu mixture she'd premade many months ago and stashed in her backpack. Throwing a generous handful into a pot of water she then set the pot on the edge of the coals and let it steep while she laid out the contents of her backpack in a sunny spot to dry.

She inventoried her food bag and her herbal supplies along with another bag that held a variety of medicines and medical supplies. She let her hands move over each container, feeling its weight, opening it and sniffing it for signs of spoilage. She drew out several bottles and choosing one, she uncapped it and gave both Sarah and Brian, a low dose of antibiotic in case their colds were more than just colds. She pulled another plastic bottle from her medicine stash and dropped two white pills into her own hand. Tylenol for pain.

Brian's cough was deep in his chest, wracking, and wet sounding. Sarah's, on the other hand, sounded dry and raspy. Either way, between the herbal tea and the antibiotic dose, she knew she should see some improvement in them both within twenty-four hours.

"Ummm, this stuff tastes like ass!" Brian

complained as he took another sip. She scowled in an attempt to look mean then laughed, finding she was unable to pull it off.

"Just drink it."

"But it tastes horrible!"

Rolling her eyes, she sighed deeply. For someone so tough, he was acting like a big baby. The man could push through four days of rain and mud, through black flies chewing on him with not one word of complaint but give him something good for him? He acted like it would kill him to finish drinking it.

"Drink it, ya big baby!" she hissed then laughed. It felt good to laugh even though doing so sent her ribs singing with pain. She watched as Brian tipped the mug up to his lips, grimace and then take another swallow. She looked over at Sarah and saw a smirk touch her mouth and shot her a warning glare.

"You too! Finish it!" she said.

Turning back to Brian, she broached the subject of staying put for the day. They needed to rest, and now that the sun had finally made an appearance, it would give them a good day to dry out their clothes, sleeping bags, and tent.

"I don't know Beth," he replied. "I'm not trying to be a hard ass here but, if what the man you killed, what he said is true, then moving on might be our wiser bet. Hell, the Bobby guy he talked about might very well be on our trail already."

He was worried. He understood what Beth wanted to do. His body screamed for a day of rest. They'd been pushing hard. But, taking even one day might be a mistake. And yes, he could set up the camp so that if this creep snuck up on them he'd have a few nasty surprises waiting but why take the chance when they didn't have to?

She sighed. She understood Brian's worry. She'd done nothing but worry these past four days. She was waiting for some boogeyman named Bobby to jump out and attack them. But she was also tired. Bone achingly tired. And she hurt. There wasn't a spot on her body that wasn't screaming with pain.

"I'm tired, Brian; you're tired, Sarah is about dead on her feet. We need to rest," she replied. She expected more of an argument from him and was surprised when he nodded.

"Okay, then. A rest day, you shall have. And if that's the plan, I'm gonna go and see if I can scrounge us up some fresh meat," he said as he downed the last of his tea.

They hadn't eaten a hot meal in days. He knew Beth's food supply was running low as well as his own. But first, before hunting, he had a few things that needed doing.

It took him only an hour or so to set up the perimeter of the camp in such a way that he felt safe, leaving the women to go hunting. Sarah did her part with the punji holes and spiked spears placed strategically into heavy thick brush cover. He'd laid a few nasty surprises of his own and showed Beth and Sarah each location so that they would get caught up in them.

While he and Sarah worked, Beth foraged in the woods for plants that she knew would be growing there. Plantain, fiddleheads, a patch of violets near a mossy tree and lastly dandelion. The greens of the dandelion would be bitter tasting but with the violet flowers, the fiddleheads and young plantain shoot to cut down on the bitterness; they would make a nice meal.

The plantain leaves she would use as a poultice for Brian's wound and the swelling and bruising on her own face and ribs. It would help to soothe the ache as well as speed the healing. She also collected white pine needles to make a tea later. White pine had a mild and soothing flavor as well as containing vitamin-C to help boost their immunity.

She took a few minutes to enjoy the quiet before she headed back to camp. She hoped Brian would get something, a rabbit, partridge or wild turkey. As hungry as she was, anything would do.

When she got back to camp, she was surprised to see Brian working with Sarah on some defensive fighting moves, and she sat on a log to watch them.

"Remember Sarah, balance. Keep moving so that you are not a static target," Brian said as he moved in on her. Beth laughed out loud as Sarah sidestepped his lunge and with a quick snap of her foot to his midsection, knocked him to the ground. He got up and brushed himself off, laughing.

"Good girl. You are getting faster," he chuckled. Turning, he dug in his pack and brought out a sharp, curved knife and handed it to Sarah. Beth's eyes widened in surprise.

"Okay, now here, here and here, " he said as he pointed to various areas on Sarah's body, "are where you want to aim for. These are areas that hold vital organs. The heart, kidney, and liver."

Sarah grinned and nodded. Beth could tell she liked this training. She watched holding her breath as Brian moved in for the attack. If Sarah slipped up and stabbed him, if he wasn't quick enough, this could end very badly.

She watched as Sarah planted her feet for balance and lashed out with the knife as Brian got closer. With a quick sidestep, he avoided the stabbing motion and moved around behind her. Sarah spun with him, not allowing him to get close enough to grab her. Brian grinned and moved quickly to the right, and Sarah once again matched him move for move.

"That is good, Sarah," he said, smiling, "you are a quick learner."

Beth was glad Brian was taking the time and interest in teaching Sarah. She thought with these little training sessions the girl's confidence would grow and perhaps even help to pull her out of the shell she'd closed herself in for far too long. After an hour or so of training, Brian finally called a halt.

"The hunting ain't gonna do itself," he said as he slung his rifle up over his shoulder. "And I don't know about you ladies, but I am getting kind'a hungry."

While he was gone, she and Sarah spent the time resting while Jessie scavenged through the woods, making crashing noises as she chased one squirrel after another. Beth noticed she didn't wander far though, coming back to the campsite panting and huffing with her tongue lolling out every few minutes as if checking on them.

Sarah was sitting near her and leaning heavily on a log dozing in the sunshine. This was just what they'd needed. This warmth, this rest. She understood Brian's concern, but he had to understand hers as well. Sometimes you need to take the time you needed, no matter if there was some kook named Bobby who might be chasing you.

Her thoughts slipped and slid through the past few weeks. The turn her life had taken and the event that landed her inside this shit show of a nightmare. She wondered if she'd bitten off more than she could chew undertaking this journey. There was no safety net under her. It was about as real and raw and dangerous as it could get.

She kept thinking about her choices, staying in New Hampshire and trying to ride it out was an option. Staying at the house filled with nothing but death was an option. She thought if she did, she too would be dead by now. Either by her hand or someone else's. No, she'd made the right decision, but would she be strong enough to stay the course was the question.

She was tired of being tired, worn out by being scared all the time. She was hungrier than she'd ever been. And her body hurt all the time, from the cold, from the pounding of her feet on the dirt and rocky trail. She was just tired of life and could see no end to this misery. Would things be better in the south? She chewed on this question over and over.

Her long and dark thoughts were interrupted by Jessie's barking, and she jumped up as she saw Brian coming up the trail toward camp. He was carrying two rabbits.

"Rabbit stew?" he said grinning as he handed her the skinned and cleaned carcasses. She was so excited that she was tempted to hug him but instead smiled and squealed happily.

"Oh my gosh! You bet!" She watched as he sat down beside Sarah and rested, his breathing sounding more labored than she liked.

"You sound worse."

"No, I feel a bit better. Must've been that horrible witch's brew you concocted," he teased. "I'm just a bit winded from the climb. I got these up on the high ridge."

She nodded, not quite believing him. Turning, she set a pot of water on to boil and threw a handful of herbs in it.

"Sorry, you're just going to have to have some more medicine," she insisted. She grinned as she heard him groan.

"Stop! It's not that bad tasting!"

He crinkled his nose and shook his head in resignation.

"Yes, dear."

She quickly set to work with her knife. Cutting the rabbits up into portions that would fit in her camp pot, she covered them with water. Adding more wood to the fire, she set the pot to boil. Once it began bubbling, she added the greens she'd collected and moved the pot to the side of the fire to simmer. She felt Brian's eyes on her as she worked, and she turned and gave him a shy smile. She saw that he'd drank the cup of tea she'd made him.

"What'cha looking at?"

"Just you. You seem comfortable cooking over an open fire. Where did you learn to do that?"

"Camping. I used to love camping." She

replied. She grew up camping with her parents, then later after she was married, she and Mitch would take long weekends away and head for the state parks. That was before her daughter was born.

"Mmmm…I camped a lot as a kid too. With my father," Brian murmured then changing the subject he asked her about Webster.

"Are we still going to try and make it there or are we moving onward up the trail?" She thought for a moment before answering and looked at Sarah. She could not see any benefit to going to town; however, they might they be able to scavenge some supplies. They might just be asking for trouble if they did. She'd seen what Hillsboro, her own town, had turned into after the event. She could only assume that all towns also imploded as Hillsboro had. Shaking her head, she grimaced. It would be too dangerous.

"Sarah, what do you think?"

Sarah shrugged her shoulders, and Beth sighed.

"No, I think we'd better just stay the course."

Brian nodded. He thought so too.

∞

The food settled in his stomach, and for the first time in days, he felt content. Relaxed, he watched Beth and Sarah as they moved about cleaning up the few dishes. Something about

Beth captured his curiosity. To him, she was an oddity. At once fragile and graceful and at the same time, he could sense an underlying toughness in this woman.

He thought about how fierce she was. Shit! The woman was beaten to a bloody mess by the men that attacked her and Sarah, and yet she hadn't given up. Each time she was knocked down by her attacker, she'd jump back up and fight some more. And yet, he'd watched her cry and sob like a child at the life she was now forced to endure. Filled with self-doubt and fear, she still forced herself day in and day out to do her very best at what life handed her.

He let his gaze set on her as she moved about the campsite. The curve of her hip, the way she held her shoulders, the movement of her hand as she gently reached over and stroked Sarah's cheek. His heart gave a strange tug, and he sighed.

Chapter Eighteen

Spike spent a wet night up on the ridge and watched as the clouds dispersed and the stars lit up the early morning sky. The air smelled of wet leaves and earth. He drew in a deep breath and settled his back against a tree. His thoughts, his anger, his pain, plagued him so that sleep eluded him. There was a deep sadness in his heart that made it difficult to catch a breath.

As darkness surrounded him, he caught himself time and time again rehashing the last few days. The blood, the carnage that greeted him as he walked through the door of his home to find his family, slaughtered. The way his beautiful wife's hair was matted with blood making it appear darker. The odd twist to her neck as she laid dead on the floor, her eyes open and staring, vacant. An ache, biting and clawing, settled deep into his soul. If hell had a word to describe it, it would be this feeling of ache and emptiness. Of a hollowness that defied tears.

Pulling himself up, he brushed the wet pine needles from the back of his pants. The first light of dawn saw him on the trail even before the sun rose. Yesterday he'd avoided the main trail on the AT, choosing to walk the ridge instead, staying high for better visibility. This morning though, he made his way down to reconnect with the AT.

He knew the men had used the main trail, and he'd followed their tracks for the past two days. He'd climbed the ridge to get above them and get a better view of the landscape. The men had taken the easiest and quickest route between towns. And they'd left plenty of evidence behind for him to follow, empty beer cans, cigarette butts, candy wrappers. Stealth he guessed was not their strong suit. Either that or they were just plain reckless and stupid. He opted for the latter.

When he came upon their dead bodies a few hours later, he cursed loudly into the silent forest. His shouts of agony and anger echoing off of the mountains. Someone had gotten to them before he could! Sinking to his knees, he hit the ground with his fists as the disappointment rocked him.

After a few minutes, he got to his feet and walked over to the first man who lay at the base of a huge pine tree. He looked down at the bullet hole that had caved in his head. The second, a large, rotund man, sported a knife wound deep into the center of his chest and the third man, well, a hole in his gut and a deep, ragged slice across his throat made short work of his sorry ass.

Whoever killed these men did a right fine job of it. He thought of the group he'd seen earlier yesterday, the man with the two women. Could they have been the ones to put these scumbags down? He pondered the question intently.

Standing up, he gazed around and noticed a fire ring. It looked like a campsite. Slowly he puzzled the pieces together of what he thought happened. The group of three, the man and the two women, were probably camping here. These guys came upon them. There was a fight, and the scumbags lost. It was simple enough to make sense. At least to him.

Their deaths didn't bring him any comfort, though. He felt robbed of the revenge he so desperately needed. With sickening nausea churning in his gut, he kicked out angrily at one of the dead men and felt his boot sink into the man's flesh. A putrid odor rose up, and he gagged as he turned his head away.

The strike of a horse's shoed hoof on a rock alerted him to movement. With his eyes on the trail, he backed silently into the thick woods and crouched down behind a thick stand of prickly brush. He brushed a mosquito from his face as he peeked through the heavy brush and waited. The campsite and the dead men were about to have some company.

He watched in morbid curiosity as four horses with riders stopped not twenty yards from where he hid. And he listened intently to their conversation.

"That's Billy, ain't it Bobby?" one of the men said as he jumped down from his horse and walked over to one of the bodies. Another man, the one he called Bobby, followed behind him.

"Yup. That's him," he said, his voice breaking with anger and pain as he gazed down upon his baby brother. His eyes filled with the sting of tears and with a dirty hand, he brushed them away and turned his face.

"Looks kinda like someone slit his throat," the first man squeaked. "And there's Tim and Elroy!"

Another of the men jumped down off of his horse and joined the first two. He stood with his hands buried deep in his pockets and a scowl on his face.

"Tim's been stabbed. Elroy was shot right between his eyes," he stated factually.

The man named Bobby bent down and examined the other two dead men and then nodded.

"Yup. Sure enough," he replied,
then coughed against the hard lump in his throat.

"Who done this?" the first man muttered. Spike watched as the man named Bobby turned to the other man, his face red with anger.

"How the hell should I know! But I will tell you this, whoever did it is gonna pay! They are gonna pay hard for killing my baby brother!" he screamed. "Mount up! We're heading back and getting the guys together. Whoever did this can't be that far ahead. We will find them!" Bobby yelled angrily. Spike watched as the men climbed back onto the horses and followed their leader back down the trail. His stomach flipped sickly with dread.

After they left, and he felt safe enough to come out of hiding, he adjusted his pack and took off down the trail heading south. His heart beat loudly in his chest, and he worked to steady his breath. He was about a day and a half behind the group he'd seen, the man and the two women. He had to warn them. Whoever Bobby was, he meant business, and he was gunning for them.

Chapter Nineteen

He traveled long into the night, cutting across deer paths, fighting thick brush and up over rough terrain, saving miles of AT under his feet. He knew this area like the back of his hand. Every side trail, every mountain, every ridge. He should; he hunted it all his life. He hunkered down for a rest beneath a scrub of dense brush beside a fallen log. Stretching his legs straight out, he eased into the darkness that cloaked him like a heavy blanket.

He gazed up at the moon, fat and bright. It was high in the night sky, and he guessed it was close to midnight. He would take a short nap, two hours at the most, and then start again. He didn't want to rest. He wanted to push on. But he knew his body wouldn't hold up to the punishment of pushing himself through the darkness. Scratches dotted his arms and face from fighting through the dense brush and low hanging branches on the trail, His muscles twitched and jumped with exhaustion.

He didn't know where this Bobby person was from, but he'd guessed it probably wasn't far from the trail. He didn't know the men he'd talked about gathering together or how many there would be. What he did know was that if he didn't warn the man and the two women and Bobby found them before he did, then they'd probably be dead within a few days.

At first light, he set out again. The sun rose above the mountains, and soon he felt the first traces of sweat tickling as it ran down his back. Their trail was easy to follow. Broken twigs as one or the other brushed by a bush on the side of the trail, moss that crushed underfoot, things that an untrained eye might not see, but he did. His years of tracking animals had trained his eyes to look for what others would not notice.

He'd come across several places where they camped and knew he wasn't long behind them — a half day at the most. Shaking his head, he grimaced. If he found it this easy to track them, then Bobby and his men would find it easy as well.

Through the long night, he'd thought about how he could help them. He would need to get them off the trail and up into the woods. They would be harder to track that way. He could bring them back to town through a series of side trails and back roads. But what then? The town was no safer for them then the trail they were on.

He thought of Roger, his grandfather. He could take them there. This thought punched him hard in the gut. The last time he'd seen Roger they'd had words. Words he now regretted.

Roger, his grandfather had built a small compound. He saw the writing on the wall, so to speak and prepared for it. And he begged Spike to move his family there when things started to go bad. But, Spike believed differently. He believed that things would smooth out, that the government would step in and help them all. That the situation wouldn't last that long. How wrong he'd been. How stupidly arrogant. And his family paid the price for his stubbornness, for his stupidity.

With a self-loathing so deep it almost made him physically sick, he pushed harder. He hadn't been able to save his family, but he might be able to save the man and the two women.

He smelled the wood smoke from their campfire just as the sky was turning from dusk to dark. He purposely made lots of noise as he got closer to their camp. He didn't want them panicking and shooting him. He froze in his tracks as a large dog came charging toward him.

"Jessie!" a female voice spoke sharply. A male voice floated out of the darkness behind him, and he turned quickly, looking into the coldest eyes he'd ever seen.

"One move and I'll be seeing your brains on the ground," the male voice growled. Spike rose his arms slowly above his head.

"I'm a friendly, mister," he said softly.

"I'll be the judge of that," the man said as

Spike felt him nudge the gun barrel into his belly.

"Turn around and walk slowly toward the camp. Remember, one wrong move, and I will shoot you."

Spike did as he was told and had no doubt this man would follow through on his threat.

The man, once he led Spike into camp, began searching him for weapons and Spike didn't resist. He would have done the same thing himself if the situation was reversed.

As he stood silent and still, his eyes met an older woman's. Although she tried to put on a brave face, he could tell she was terrified. Behind her stood a younger girl, if he had to guess, he'd say she was barely sixteen. Both looked travel weary. The older woman showed dark bruises on her face and eyes, purple that had taken on a shade of sickly yellow. She'd been beaten. Spike wondered if it was the dead men back yonder that did it. The younger girl was scrawny, hungry looking. But nowadays, most people he saw looked the same, malnourished and near starvation.

Mother and daughter? He didn't know why, but he didn't think they were related. It was just a feeling in his gut. He hadn't gotten a good look at the man yet, but from within the light of the shadows, he guessed him to be at least six foot tall with a wiry build: broad shoulders and thick arms.

"Okay, sit down," the man said as he pushed him roughly toward a log near the fire. Spike sat as the man told him to. The man sat across the fire, facing him with his gun resting on his knees aimed right toward him. His finger, Spike noticed, lay alongside the trigger. In a safe position but one that would give him split-second access if he needed to pull it.

"So you must be Bobby, man I don't know, but dang, I somehow thought you'd be, say, bigger?" the man said then laughed softly. Spike smiled in return, then couldn't help but burst out laughing.

"So you know about Bobby?" he snickered between gusts of laughter. "Sorry dude, no, I am not Bobby. I'm the man that's gonna save your asses from Bobby though."

∞

Sarah watched from across the fire. She could see, no she could feel that the man who sat across from her was a good man. His body language, his voice, even his eyes spoke of kindness. Dark hair, a dimple on the left side of his mouth when he laughed, green eyes, yes, she thought him quite handsome. Getting up, she walked around the fire pit and sat down beside him, ignoring Beth's hard stare. She blushed when he turned his head toward her and smiled. It was an impish smile, one that could only come from someone with a sense of humor.

She always had a gift of reading people. And most times she was right in her assessment of them. Like Beth. She'd read Beth as being kind and gentle. Naïve, actually, and that's why she chose to stay with her. That is why she felt that Beth needed her. And Brian, she read him as tough, hard when he needed to be, but loyal and fierce with those he cared about. And she knew he cared for her and Beth.

This man. He carried a lot of pain; she saw it in the shadow that lay just behind his eyes. But he meant them no harm. Satisfied with her assessment, she sat with her hands folded in her lap and listened to the conversation unfold.

Chapter Twenty

Roger Boyslin shook his head and groaned in frustration. At sixty-six years old he felt he'd seen way too much of life. First Viet Nam, now this. Reaching over, he grabbed Cain's shoulder and squeezed tight.

"Don't worry, boy. We'll go get him," The 'him' he was talking about was his grandson, Spike. The damn fool had taken off on his own to track down the men who murdered his wife and children, Roger's great-grandchildren.

When Spike came to him, just after it happened, his frame of mind was almost maniacal, psychotic. He talked of the butchery through choking tears and sobs. He talked of hunting down the men and skinning them alive for what they did to his family. Roger tried to talk him out of his crazy plan and thought he had only to find out; the man decided to go it alone anyway. What Spike failed to hear was that those three men were part of a larger gang from a few towns over. That this gang was heavily armed and dangerous. That he, Spike, would not have a prayer in hell of winning if he took them on alone.

Roger begged him to wait. To give him the time to gather up his men, plan and approach this with a level head. But Spike refused to listen. In his grief, his heart was hell-bent on revenge.

Roger knew about the gang for quite some time now. They had raided the town several times, always leaving behind a trail of bodies whenever they showed their faces.

"Why didn't he just wait for us!" Cain grumbled. Roger shook his head. He knew why Spike hadn't waited. It was the same reason he'd refused to move his family to the protective shelter of the compound: stubbornness, pride, and downright hard headedness. His grandson, although he loved him dearly, could be a pisser when he chose to.

"Gather up the men. Tell them we need to move in five minutes," Roger said as he pulled on a pair of old, beat up work boots. Pain ripped through his shoulder as he bent to tie the laces. Bursitis: an old man's ailment, and it sucked to be getting old.

He hadn't wanted to take the fight to the enemy, but Spike's move left him no choice. He'd planned to lie in wait, to plan and execute a defensive strategy.

He knew they would have a better chance at success if fought on their own turf. He didn't know how large the gang out of Massachusetts was. He'd heard rumors of thirty men up to one hundred. He'd been gathering intel slowly over the past few weeks from his network but still didn't have a good handle on the size of the gang's numbers.

What he did know was this; these men, this gang that Spike was aiming for was part of a much larger group that called themselves the Tristate Alliance. His connections out of the south were tracking these criminals and what they were relaying back scared the living shit out of Roger.

From what he learned, this group was the culmination of three other gangs which grew their numbers to a staggering amount. Where ever they went, they left destruction and death in their wake. What he didn't get was an accurate count on the force they'd become. And this bothered him. In Nam he'd gone into enough fights to know, you never underestimate the numbers of your opponents. That mistake could cost you the battle and many lives.

He'd seen the writing on the wall years before the virus spread like a prairie fire through the United States. He knew something would befall his great nation. He just hadn't known what that something was. He'd prepared though. Stockpiling food, fuel, medicine, ammunition, and whatever else he thought would get them through. He'd created underground caches and root cellars, he'd dug several wells on his property, raised herds of goats and cows, pigs, horses, and mules. He'd raised flocks of chickens, turkeys, ducks, and geese.

Mary Anne, his wife, spent hours each day in the kitchen, canning, drying, preserving. Then he began building out-buildings under the guise of animal housing so the town wouldn't catch wind of his prepping activities. These outbuildings though, were for human inhabitants. Little tiny homes equipped with gravity fed water from the well, solar panels for energy, woodstoves for cooking and heat.

It took him many years to build his compound, and less than two months to fill it with carefully selected people. He hadn't done this all on his own though. Others believed the same as he did. And those others were the foundation of the militia. They were a skilled group.

At his compound there were seventy fighting men and their families at last count, and every day they were training up new fighters to strengthen their position. Several compounds they'd connected with boasted numbers far larger. They had a communications system that reached as far north as Canada and as far west as California.

They were the Truth Seekers, and as a group, they kept constant information flowing. And thus far they had been able to hold their own against the onslaught of trouble that frequented their doorsteps.

He remembered when their little group of

fifteen started. It was years of planning and preparations, communicating theories that hadn't come to fruition and watching the ever failing government policies. They now kept in contact through HAM radio. The information they all shared was crucial to each of their success.

The original fifteen of them once were part of a much larger group but broke off and formed their own after internal strife, bickering, and power struggles. Accusations of fear-mongering and spreading conspiracy theories finally drove them out to form their own group. And now they had compounds throughout the United States.

In the Northeast, there was Naomi Silter, who established her compound in New Hampshire. In Kentucky, there was Alan Moses's compound that at last count was three hundred strong. Then in Wisconsin, there was Joe Nagler. He'd been the founder of their core group.

Then there was Joyce Mclista, a spunky ball of fire from Alabama, who had a compound that ran like a well-oiled machine. She kept them apprised of the activity going on in her neck of the woods. Kelly Durham ran her compound out of Ontario, Canada and she was their ears to the North, keeping them all apprised of the refugee and border activity.

Seth Pinley was located in Central

Kentucky. He and Alan worked closely with each other, being the largest of all the compounds. They formed several offshoot compounds throughout their state, taking in refugees from all over the nation, training them and working on trade specialty classes that brought up a well-educated network of skilled carpenters, blacksmiths, welders and various other trade skills long forgotten by the current society.

In California, the first state to be hit with the virus, there was Claude Underwood. He had the toughest go of all. As a highly skilled Registered Nurse, retired military, and well educated Crisis Responder, he had to keep most of his prepping activities from those around him.

California had been spiraling down long before the event. Too much corruption, too many that couldn't conceive of the shit show that was coming and too many laws that would restrict the people from doing what he was doing, prepping for the end of the world. The struggle for Claude to create and build the compound in his part of the nation was fraught with one disaster after another.

The Gun ban made him a criminal, then the cost of living so high that investing the money nearly broke him. But, with the help of the group, he persevered and got it up and running successfully.

Taylor Eddie hailed from Florida; his compound ran alongside another set of patriots called the Gator Swamp Militia. After several rough and bumpy encounters, power struggles, and skirmishes, the two groups pulled together on common ground and settled into combining their resources to form the Coastal Patriots; a diverse and highly skilled and scattered network that ran the full length of the Eastern Coast.

Lastly, there were Kelsey Salmiver, who was from Arizona, and Lori Franks, from Tennessee; both women brought the skill of communications to the entire group They became the bones of th HAM radio communication network. In the early days of planning they shipped equipment, instructed, and educated on the what's, where's, and how's of the HAM radio world. They were the planners; mapping out escape routes for each member should they have to bug out, setting up safe houses, creating drop locations for supplies and other needed items. They were the planners; mapping out escape routes for each member should they have to bug out, setting up safe houses, creating drop locations for supplies and other needed items.

Jenny Sigmond hailed from the great state of Texas. She was key in keeping them all apprised of the border activities; the military movements and the reformation of territories that were constantly shifting and changing hands with each new player in the game. Lisa Belmore and Kay Thibalt were part of her offshoot group, each creating mirroring compounds in their areas and thus building a massive defense system that could be implemented within a moment's notice should they need to move quickly from one compound to another.

Then came Earl Vorhees, out of Mississippi. His compound was only a hundred or so strong, but it was growing fast, and he was active in planting the seeds of smaller, interconnected groups of patriots in neighboring states.

Kris Gallerger built his compound in the cold climate of Minnesota. Spread out on one hundred and fifty acres with roughly seventy-five or so fighting men; Kris had one advantage that most of the others did not, his compound was surrounded with highly trained ex-military. His group fought weekly, sometimes daily, skirmishes with gangs that came in hordes from the nearby cities.

To say they'd all been busy the past few years would be an understatement. Roger thought of this and grimaced. They all saw the future and it scared them shitless.

They were sitting better than most. Reports through the network brought them news of cities, towns and little one-stoplight burgs decimated by looting and burning.

Nightmarish stories of cannibalism and violence that could even make the most hardened of men weep in despair. They were waging war, one against the very own people of the country who wanted nothing more than to see it fall.

The biggest fight for him was the onset of martial law. When the suits came and tried to pilfer supplies from his compound for the FEMA camps they opened, he'd been prepared for that as well. They brought plenty of firepower with them; the fight was bloody and swift. He'd lost several good men, but they lost more. Then, shortly after, the camps petered out; the suits disappeared along with their soldiers.

Martial law turned into no law other than the law of survival. It was then that the gangs began to spring up in the surrounding areas. Each gang leader was trying to establish their turf. Skirmishes were fought, lives were lost, kingpins rose above the cesspool like scum on a pond — survival of the fittest, of the meanest in a jungle of Screwed Seven Way's to Sunday.

The winter was hard on his compound. They lost a few, some to illnesses, some from accidents, and violence. But they made it. They worked to help the townspeople the best they could, taking many into the compound while others, such as his grandson, adamantly insisted on going it alone.

This presented another problem for him and his men. Those who lived outside the compound were defenseless. So, nightly patrols were sent out to try and keep the area safe. But this spread his men thin. Exhaustion set in and mistakes were made, so he pulled back on assisting, realizing he had to take care of his own first and foremost.

If trouble arrived and he knew about it, he would send out a small contingency to help put it down. But often by the time he heard about it, the damage was already done, and they were too late. Spikes situation was a prime example of arriving too late to help.

Pulling on his rain jacket, Roger sighed deeply and opened the door. It was time to find his grandson and shed some blood.

Chapter Twenty-One

Bobby seethed with anger. His baby brother was dead, and the monster that killed him would pay dearly. He pushed his way through the door and slammed it behind him. He'd dropped Harris off with the instruction to pull the men together and have them ready to meet within the hour so they could lay plans to leave. He thought an early morning start would be the best option; that way, his men would have time to prepare for what might turn into a trip of several days.

He didn't care if he had to track Billy's killer to the end of the earth, he would find whoever it was, and their screams would be heard far and wide. His mind spun with ideas of how they would pay as he strutted jerkily back and forth through the house. His moves were frantic and frenzied as his state of mind became more and more agitated.

No, he wouldn't kill them right away. That was too good for them. He'd make whoever did this suffer for a long, long time. And he was becoming very good at inflicting suffering. Walking over to his desk, he opened the drawer and pulled out a small baggie of white powder. Slipping a small line on the dark, oak top of the desk, he rolled up a one dollar bill and placed it in one nostril then snorted deeply. The burn made his eyes water, then glass over as the cocaine began working its magic. Slumping in the chair, he leaned back and closed his eyes. A contented sigh passed through his thin lips.

Billy had been his sidekick, his shotgun bro. All his life, Bobby had looked out for his baby brother. And the pain kicked him square in the gut. His eyes filled with tears, and he angrily wiped them away. Yeah, the kid wasn't the brightest pumpkin in the patch, often making stupid decisions that landed him in hot water, but Bobby had always bailed him out. He'd always protected him.

Before the event hit, Billy had been a gangly, clumsy kid. No girlfriend, no real friends to speak of. He was shy, introverted, and unsure of himself. But after the event, Bobby watched him grow and blossom. His confidence had exploded as he took one woman after another and satiated his twisted needs, sometimes at the rate of two or three times a day. Bobby taught him how to shoot a gun, how to ride a horse, how to be a man. The crooked little boy grin disappeared with the boy he'd been, and a cruel and sardonic twist took its place. His younger brother was feared and respected.

Growing up with parents as they had, if they hadn't looked out for each other, then neither would have survived. For someone to kill him, to slit his throat, and leave him on the side of the trail for the animals to eat was just too much for Bobby's mind, and he sank to his knees as grief and anger washed over him.

A soft hand on his shoulder penetrated his pain, and turning, he pulled Tamara into him. Like an infant, he cried on her shoulder as she held him tight. The smile on her face was cold as the winter snow just starting to melt. She gazed out the window, all the while, her hands rubbing his back.

She hated this man, hated him more than she'd ever hated anyone before. She'd go to her grave cursing him, but she'd take him with her. Not only did he use her as his punching bag and mattress, but she also was the maid and the cook. And as the cook, well, she just loved the extra little touches she put into his food.

Slowly he'd been feeling the effects of those little touches; cramping, diarrhea, bouts of blurred vision, rapid heartbeat. He'd complained to her about it, and she'd convinced him it was from the drugs and the heavy drinking and cigarettes; but she knew what it was.

Her secret weapon would send him painfully to his grave eventually; not fast enough for her satisfaction, but every day she knew she was killing him just a little bit more and this made what he did to her bearable. By adding just a few scant drops of Belladonna into his food, his morning coffee, his beer at night, she was slowly poisoning him. Her smile widened.

The men grumbled softly, the sound reverberating through the small living room, and Bobby shouted for them to simmer the hell down. He drew in a deep breath. Silence, as thick as fog, settled over the room. His shoulders tensed as he launched into his plan.

"Be prepared to stay gone for a few days. We are going to find who killed my brother!" he spat angrily. "And then we are gonna have us a little old-fashioned justice! No one gets away with hurting our brothers, no one!"

Harris stood up and looked at Bobby. He didn't like the idea of the entire group going after one man and leaving their interests unprotected. He said this to Bobby, suggesting he take only a few men to hunt down Billy's killer.

Bobby turned to him and scowled angrily, his eyes glaring.

"I don't care what you think! Sit down and shut up!" He watched as Harris, red-faced, sat back down. There were times he hated Bobby, and this was one of those times.

"We are going in two groups. Harris will be leading one, and I'll be leading the other," he explained. "My group will stick to the AT and surrounding towns, Harris, you and your boys will be taking the side trails and skirting above us. If this person is anywhere in the area, we will catch em'."

With that set, he went on to instruct the men where and when to meet up the next morning. At meeting end, as everyone filtered out the door into the darkness, Bobby grabbed Harris's arm and pulled him aside. How dare his second in command question him? It was time to show Harris just who was boss of this shit show.

He swung hard, and a feeling of satisfaction rushed through him as he felt the bite of his knuckles land squarely on Harris' jaw, knocking him back. He stood nose to nose with him and screamed into his face, spittle splattering Harris' skin with every word. He held a knife to his throat, applying just enough pressure to make Harris' eyes widen in fear.

"Do you wanna get cut asshole? Do ya?" Harris shook his head in fear as Bobby's eyes stared deep into his.

"Then you never, ever disrespect me again in front of the men! Do I make myself clear?"

Harris nodded again. "Crystal. It won't happen again, boss," he said as he cowered under Bobby's hateful, murderous stare.

"Get the hell out of my sight before I kill you just for the hilly hell fun of it!" he spat as he drew the knife away and shoved Harris toward the door.

Breathing heavily to calm himself, he yelled for Tamara to bring him a beer. His plan was a good one, and it irked the shit out of him that Harris disagreed. How dare he do that? What did that asshole know anyway? He'd been nothing but a two-bit punk before Bobby pulled him into the gang and gave him the status of second in command. And this was how he repaid him? Seething anger coursed through his body and he clenched his fists to keep his hands from shaking.

The cowardly shit! The more he thought of it, the angrier he became. He should have sliced his throat. He should have just let his blade sink deep into the pasty white skin and watched as the blood flowed over it. It would have served as a lesson to others never to cross him, never to question his authority. And he'd be rid of the backstabbing coward once and for all.

With a shaking hand, he pulled his knife from its leather sheath and rubbed his thumb lightly across the blade, watching as a thin line of blood appeared. Lifting his thumb to his mouth, he sucked gently and tasted the metallic, salty thickness of blood as it coated his tongue. He was in a murderous kind of mood. And he needed to hurt someone.

Tamara grabbed the beer from the fridge and popped the top. Glancing over her shoulder to see if the coast was clear, she added a generous dose of poison. Pasting a smile on her face, she walked in and handed it to Bobby.

"Here, ya go," she said softly. She saw the dark anger on his face and took a step back. He was in a mood, and this usually meant a hard night for her.

"Bobby? What's wrong?" she asked quietly. He glared at her coldly and held up his knife.

"I'm in the mood to kill someone, sweetheart," he said, then smiled a bitter smile. Tamara lowered her eyes and began to pray. And strangely enough, it was a prayer for him to kill her and be done with it finally. She wanted out of this life. She wanted to go home.

Chapter Twenty-Two

Spike savored every bite of the rabbit stew. Beth did a good job flavoring it up with a few herbs. The broth was rich and soothing, and as he sipped the last few drops from his bowl, he sighed with contentment.

Sarah and Beth had long turned in for the night. He and Brian sat quietly by the fire, watching it burn low as they talked. He filled Brian in on how he came to be up here on the AT, how he was following and hunting the three men Brian and Beth killed, and lastly, how he knew about Bobby and his plans to hunt Brian, Sarah, and Beth down and make them pay for killing Billy, his younger brother. It was a long story, but Brian listened intently to every word the man said.

His hunger satiated, he put the cup bowl on the ground and stared across the fire at Brian. He picked up a rock and slowly tossed it from hand to hand. He was tired, and he felt that tiredness in every muscle of his body. He watched, mesmerized, as the light and shadows played off of Brian's arms, highlighting then darkening a series of tattoos. He knew those tats. He'd seen many in his years as a cop. The man had done time.

"So what prison was you in?"

Brian raised his eyes to Spikes and grinned. He wondered when this former cop would ask.

"Southern State Correctional in Springfield, Vermont." Spike raised his eyebrows. He was impressed. That was a Federal Prison.

"What was your sentence?"

Brian smiled coldly at the dance that began between them and wondered how long it would take for Spike to connect the dots.

"Life."

"Whew man! That's rough," Spike said softly. Life in a federal prison meant only one thing. This man was one badass dude. The cop-killing, murdering kind of badass dude.

"How many?"

"More than I can count," Brian replied.

Spike thought for a moment, pondering what he'd said.

"What is your last name, Brian?"

"Pittman."

He felt his stomach clench with horror, and he sucked in a deep breath before letting it out in a whoosh. He looked at Brian with a wary expression on his face. The man across from him was once considered the most dangerous of men in the Tri-State area. His list of victims was long and bloody.

"Brian, the Butcher," he muttered. "They

took you down in Boston, right?"

"Yup! Nice to make your acquaintance," Brian said, then laughed as he saw his reputation was still intact. Yes, he was a killer. Dubbed Brian the Butcher by the media after he'd left a score of bodies in his wake. So many bodies that even he lost count. But not one of the men he killed hadn't deserved it.

"I followed your trial. I don't know of a cop in the northeast that hadn't," Spike said softly.

"Don't believe everything you hear. Sometimes when justice can't be served through our so-called system, then it has to be served by someone like me," Brian replied. He'd make no excuses, and he'd not explain his actions nor apologize for what he'd done.

"Just don't kill me in my sleep you rat bastard," Spike teased then laughed. Him, a cop, sworn to uphold the law, trying to save the ass of a hardcore criminal from other hardcore criminals. It was a bloody laughable Greek tragedy. Sighing tiredly, he shot a grin across the fire at Brian.

"Umm, not that I don't trust you, man, which by the way I don't, but I think I'll take the first watch if you don't mind."

Brian grinned in reply. He found himself liking this man that sat across from him. At least he had a bit of a sense of humor. He hoped he wouldn't have to one day kill him.

They talked long into the night, and Spike filled him in on the best route of travel. Filled him in on his grand-fathers compound/farm and that they would find safe sanctuary there. Brian agreed and listened intently. The man had a good head on his shoulders.

"So, I think we should leave as soon as the first light hits. Bobby and his men have horses, so they will have the advantage of crossing the miles faster than we can on foot. But, if we stick to side trails and bushwhacking, it'll be harder for them to follow. You, being the elusive bastard you are, will be covering our tracks as we go," Spike said.

Brian laughed softly. Yes, he was elusive, the military taught him that. And how to erase any evidence so that even the best trackers wouldn't be able to follow. Nodding in agreement, he had to admit; Spike had a good plan. At least it would give them a fighting chance.

"These guys, how bad are they?" Brian asked.

Spike shook his head, and his eyes hardened as images of his wife and children flitting across his mind. In normal times, these punks would be nothing to worry about, but now that there were no laws to stop them?

"Well, let's say this. Those two ladies? If Bobby and his men get their hands on them? Then death would be a blessing. You'd be better off mercy killing them before that happens. And if things go bad, I hope to God you do," he whispered as he thought of what they did to his family. Those animals massacred his wife. They did unspeakable, unimaginable things to her before they'd killed her. The thought crashed into his heart like a sledgehammer, driving pain deep into gut.

"Then it sounds like we'd just better not let that happen," Brian growled. He'd met men like this Bobby before. Rabid dogs who needed putting down. He pulled his knife from its sheath and grabbed his stone from the side pocket of his pack. Slowly, with a steady hand, he ran the blade across the stone. Spike watched as the light from the fire danced off of the metal of the blade, and a chill ran down his spine. He'd heard horror stories of what Brian did with a knife. Stories that made his skin crawl with revulsion. Turning his eyes away, he said softly,

"We won't." And Brian could tell by the set of his jaw, the pain in his eyes that Spike would stay true to his word.

As Spike took the first watch, he stoked the fire and settled in for a long four hours. Jessie curled up beside him, and he ran his hand through her fur as his mind drifted. He felt the calm rhythm of her breathing as he absently stroked her back and sides. The black sky was filled with a carpet of stars and the moon, receding in its fullness cast an eerie glow into the darkness that surrounded him. He listened to the night sounds around him. The breaking of branches as deer, bear and other nocturnal creatures stirred about.

The air smelled sharply of pine and wood smoke. If it hadn't been for the horror of the past few days, he thought he might truly enjoy this night. It was too a long time since he'd been camping. This peacefulness, this contentedness was just a cruel illusion. The world had changed. His world had changed. There would be no more fun camping trips with his wife and kids. There would be no more pizza's and movies as the four of them cuddled up on the couch, him on one end, the kids in the middle and his wife on the other end with a bowl of popcorn between them. That life was gone. It would never be back, and this thought coldly shattered any illusions he had.

He sighed as he scratched at the many black fly bites on his neck. They itched like holy hell. He hated spring just for the fact that it seemed to give birth to all the biting and stinging things. And he was finding out quickly, all those biting and stinging things weren't just the bothersome insects. A lot of them were men and women who crawled out of the winters darkness and cold, birthing to a new season of death and destruction.

A cop and a killer. Two women and a dog. An event that changed his entire world. His life had taken so many twists and turns these past months that it left him wondering. Why he was even still alive and still breathing through this nightmare. Everything he'd loved, everything that mattered was gone. What was left for him out there?

Revenge… That's what was left. He'd help Brian, Sarah and Beth get to a safer place. Then his life's mission, his only purpose, would be to exact his revenge on those who'd given reign to the men that took his everything.

A pain so deep and still surrounded his heart as dark and thick as the smoke rising from the campfire. Bitter and acrid, cloying, and consuming. Leaning back against the log he was using as a backrest, he closed his eyes and let his emotions sweep through him. Although alive he felt a shell of the man he'd once been. Hollowed out with only the bitter taste of sorrow that threatened to shatter him.

Chapter Twenty-Three

After a quick breakfast of leftover rabbit stew, the group started over the rough terrain of deer trails and rocky outcrops. Spike led them toward the ridgeline. A place where he would have the advantage of clear view for miles around. Sarah fell in behind him, followed by Beth and then lastly; Brian brought up the rear.

Within an hour of traveling the sun peeked up over the mountains and Beth could already tell the day was going to be hot. Sweat rolled down her back, soaking her shirt, and her breath sounded wheezy as she struggled against the rough trail.

Pushing ahead trying to keep up the pace, they burned miles under their hot feet. Through tangled underbrush that tripped them up, over rocky outcrops that tore into the soles of their boots and drove pain deep into their legs. They were fighting the black flies, fighting the horse flies. Fighting for every breath as they climbed higher and higher.

"We will need to refill our water bottles," she hollered, stopping on the trail and placing her hands on her knees as she bent to catch her breath. Ahead, Spike turned and nodded.

"There's a stream not too much further

ahead. We can fill our water bottles there."

Looking over her shoulder, she noticed that Brian fell quite a bit behind, and she motioned for everyone to stop. His cough, although better, was still there and his breathing wasn't one hundred percent yet. When he caught up, he gave her a quizzical look.

"Why'd you stop?"

"Because I was waiting for you to catch up."

"Don't. You keep pushing ahead. I'll be right behind you guys. I'm covering our trail," he explained between panting breaths as he leaned against a tree.

"We're pushing too hard. You won't be able to keep this pace up, Brian. "

"I'll keep up. We've got to keep pushing," he replied in annoyance. A sheen of sweat glistened on his face red with exertion.

"Okay. Whatever!" she snapped as she turned and stomped away from him up the hill. He saw Spike raise an eyebrow in question and he shook his head. Best to just let it go. They were all tired and irritated. The punishing, grueling trek was starting to take its toll on their moods.

He hadn't told either her or Sarah what Spike told him about the men that were chasing them. Not the gory details. He didn't want to scare them any more than they already were. But these men, Bobby's gang, were similar to so many gangs that he had dealings with in the past. They were ruthless, they were violent, and once they had their eyes set on a course, it would take nothing short of blood and bullets to stop them.

Beth could hear the river up ahead and picked up her pace. She was as parched as a dirt hill, and sweat rolled in itchy little trickles down between her shoulder blades. The sun overhead, cut shadows in and out of the trees dappling the ground beneath her.

"Okay guys, let's fill up here," Spike said. She sighed in relief and shrugged her sore shoulders out of her pack and threw it on the ground. Stretching, she groaned as one muscle after another released tension.

It was a small, fast flowing brook that cut through and down to the Housatonic River. Spike fished here many times as a boy with his grandfather and later, by himself as an adult.

The water was clean, fast flowing, and crystal clear. Spike watched as Beth walked to the river's edge.

"Be careful Beth. The water is moving at a good clip," he warned. She shot him a nod over her shoulder before taking off her hiking boots, stripping out of her sticky tee shirt and wading into the cold water up to her knees. The current did its best to unbalance her.

Bending over, she cupped her hands and splashed her face, shoulders, and neck then dampened her hair. Damn, she was hot and the icy water, although shocking, felt wonderful on her skin. Turning her head, she watched as Sarah moved up beside her and did the same.

"It's a hard hike, huh?"

Sarah nodded tiredly.

"Are you okay? Do we need to stop and rest awhile?"

Sarah shook her head.

"Okay, but you tell me if you need to," she said softly. As she rinsed her shirt in the water and put it back on, she cut an irritated glance toward Spike. It angered her that he and Brian were pushing them so hard. Yes, she knew that both men were worried about this Bobby creep and his cohorts following them and she was as well but pushing themselves to the point of collapse wouldn't help their cause.

When Brian moved up beside her, she snapped at him.

"You've got to tell Spike to slow down. He's pushing too hard. It's not doing us any good if we collapse on the trail." Brian shook his head in frustration and anger.

"Look, Beth, I don't know what you don't get about these men that are after us. They are killers! They are not nice people that you can reason with. We killed one of theirs; now they want to kill us!" he growled. "If we slow down and they catch up to us then...." he didn't continue and let his words stay unspoken. She didn't get it. Or she refused to get it. He wasn't sure which.

"I know! Don't you think I know? For God's sake, it was me and Sarah that were attacked by the brother of those animals!" she spat back at him, her eyes flashing with anger as she fought against the rising anger and having a total meltdown. "I'm not as stupid as you seem to believe I am but tell me this Sherlock! How are we going to fight them if we are too exhausted even to lift our guns if they do catch up to us? Huh? Look at you? You can't even catch a good breath! And Sarah? Both of you have been sick, and with only one day of rest, you can't heal. I am not saying we turtle crawl, but we're not up to running a marathon to the Connecticut border either!"

Brian laughed in surprise and shook his head. Who'd a thought it; this gentle, sweet little Beth had such a temper. Turning to Spike, he muttered,

"We gotta slow down, man," then he grinned. "She's the boss and to be honest; I'm kind'a afraid of her. Spike laughed out loud, then nodded.

"Sure thing bro. Yeah, I hear ya."

They pushed on until the sun was nearly set. Mosquitoes ravaged them by the hordes, swarming black clouds that couldn't be slapped away no matter how hard they tried. By the time they set up camp, they all were exhausted, frustrated, itchy with bug bites and hungry but too tired to do anything more than chew on a few pieces of jerky from Brian's stash. While Sarah and Beth went off into the woods to relieve themselves, Brian gathered sticks and logs for a fire. Spike set up the tent.

"I'll take the first watch," Brian said as he pulled a downed log toward the fire to use as a backrest, coughing the whole time. He grimaced with each cough as pain ripped through his lungs and chest. Spike nodded.

"We've covered some good miles, today, man. If we can do the same tomorrow, we should almost be able to reach the Connecticut border. Then from there, Rogers compound is only a few short miles down the road."

Brian sighed tiredly. His chest was once again hurting, and each breath felt like fire in his lungs.

"I think I've got pneumonia," he muttered quietly so Beth and Sarah wouldn't overhear him.

Spike groaned. "Are you gonna be able to make the miles tomorrow?"

"I have no choice," Brian snapped tiredly.

And he didn't. He'd ask Beth to fix him another cup of that witches brew he hated so much and for some more of the antibiotic she gave him earlier. It helped ease the congestion in his chest yesterday, and for a few hours after drinking the tea and taking medicine, he'd felt better.

He raised his finger to his lips when he heard Sarah and Beth coming back. Spike nodded that he understood. He didn't know Beth much at all; just what little she'd told him about herself, but he could see, she had a strong, bossy personality. If she even suspected Brian was as sick as he was, she'd throw a fit and make them take a rest day. And that would be, in his opinion, a very dangerous thing to do. They couldn't afford the luxury of resting. Not with Bobby and his gang after them.

Chapter Twenty-Four

Beth sat by the fire and pulled the knife from her belt to chop up the partridge that Spike bagged from his early morning hunt. The sky turned from purplish black to gray. She'd gotten up early, and so did Spike. Brian napped. Both men were tired from guard duty, and Beth decided that tonight, she and Sarah would take shifts so they could sleep.

"Is that a turkey carving knife?" Spike asked.

Beth nodded. "Yup."

She heard him laugh and scowled at him.

"You are serious? That is a carving knife?" he choked between gusts of laughter as his eyes filled with tears. A carving knife. What the hell was this woman thinking?

Irritated, she didn't see the humor. "Yes, I told you it was."

"Okay, so why a carving knife? What, did ya steal it from someone's kitchen?"

She shook her head. "No, it was mine. It was the sharpest knife in my rack, so I brought it with me." This thought brought her glaringly back to the day the turkey carving knife saved her life. The blood, the shards of glass, the pain of the burns on her arms. A shiver danced down her spine, and she pushed the memory away. It was a memory she wasn't willing to share. Staring down at her hands, she muttered under her breath. They were filthy with grit from the trail, covered with callouses and healed blisters. This saddened her. Her hands used to be soft and pretty. Nails always perfectly filed to shape and adorned with polish. A cough and snicker from Spike brought her out of her thoughts.

She saw him shake his head and smirk. She couldn't help but grin.

Beth was a mystery to him, and Spike cut his eyes to her watching as she continued chopping up the partridge to toss into the pot. Most people had buck knives. Not her. She carried a long, sharp turkey carving knife tucked in her belt. Well, he supposed it was better than nothing. Brian, hearing the laughter and conversation, smiled and cut his eyes at Spike.

"Hey, it's served us well so far, so don't laugh too hard," he said.

Spike nodded.

"Yup, now to find a wild turkey for that long ass knife she's carrying," he teased.

Beth laughed. "Don't you have something to do?" she snickered.

"Yes, ma-am. I do," he replied with a grin and pulled himself up off of the ground just as Sarah came sleepily stumbling out of the tent.

"Morning sunshine," he said as he strolled past her. Sarah grimaced and shot him a dark look at which he just laughed. She was not an early morning person, but she had the most beautiful blue eyes he'd ever seen.

With breakfast over, they all set to breaking down camp. Brian worked on erasing any evidence of them being there just in case Bobby or his men came through the area. Backpacks on they began to once again push through heavy scrub brush and climb steep hills.

The sun rose bright, its heat already felt in the morning air as it beat fiercely down on them. The AT, a worn and well-used trail would have been an easier hike by far. But easier wasn't always better. And in their case, easier would mean more dangerous.

She let her mind wander as her feet pounded the dirt and rocky trail they were following. Spike said they could make it to the Connecticut border by late afternoon. She hoped so. From there he'd said it was only a few short miles of dirt road to his grandfather's compound where they would find safety and rest. She wondered what this compound was like and moved up beside Spike. Sarah stayed in step right beside her.

"So tell me about your grandfather's place."

Spike smiled and wiped away beads of sweat from his forehead with the back of his hand.

"Ahhh the Belcher Homestead. You'll

love it there," he said. "Grandpa bought the farm before I was born. One hundred and fifty acres of woods and fields. Run down barns and sheds. It was a mess. He and Gram spent years working the land, tearing down the old buildings and building new ones, planting big gardens, putting up fences and bringing in animals. Mainly chickens, ducks, geese, pigs, goats, and cows. They brought in horses too."

He smiled as he remembered the old homestead. "After I was born and old enough to help, mom and dad would bring me to the homestead and turn me loose with grandpa. As a kid, I thought it was the greatest thing of all. But as I got older, not so much. So I went there less and less."

She saw a shadow of sadness darken his eyes, and she nodded. She understood less and less — more than he knew.

"I hadn't realized what Grandpa did to the old homestead. Not until about two years ago, before the event. At first, I thought he was crazy. Turning into one of those nutbag prepper coots. But now, God now I wished to hell I'd stuck around. I wished to hell I had paid attention." Beth nodded. She too wished she'd paid more attention to the world around her. Perhaps then she would have made an effort to learn those things she so sorely needed now. Skills such as hunting and trapping. Learning to can and preserve her food, or how to build a smokehouse or even an outhouse. How to shoot a gun and break it down to clean it. How to start a fire without the convenience of a lighter or matches. There was so much she could have learned to better prepare herself for this new life.

"So how many people at his compound?" she asked. Curiosity tickled her. She'd only read about these prepper groups or compounds and found the idea of seeing a real one captivating.

"I don't know. I haven't been there since before the event. But I do know this. He's got enough food, fuel and other supplies stocked up in that place to last years. He's got enough men and firepower to hold off an army. He wanted me and my family to go there when things started turning to shit, but I was too stubborn, too stupid to take him up on his offer. And now…" he trailed off weakly.

"Now it is what it is," she stated firmly. He looked at her gratefully and nodded. She was right. It was what it was. There was no turning back the clocks so he could go and fix everything he screwed up. There was no bringing his sons or his wife back from the dead. There was just this. Right here, right now.

"I can't wait to get there. I want to rest. To not be looking over my shoulder constantly and worried about whether or not we're gonna get attacked around the next bend." she replied tiredly.

This compound he spoke of, his

grandfather's homestead, sounded like a little piece of heaven in this hell they were living in. Beside her, Sarah nodded in agreement and slid her small hand into Beth's. Beth looked down at her and smiled tiredly. This journey so far was hard on the child. From feet battered by blisters to a body battered by the men in her life, Beth thought it was a miracle that Sarah survived at all. She was one tough chic for sure.

The sunlight bounced off her dark hair, making it shimmer and shine. She couldn't get over how beautiful Sarah was. Eyes sometimes the color of crystal blue sky and other times, changing to a darker and deeper shade of blue that reminded her of the sky during an afternoon thunderstorm. Wild and volatile, depending on her mood.

Yesterday they'd had the luxury of a poor man's bath in the river, where they both washed their hair in the cold water with the bar soap that she tucked in her pack. Even Jessie decided to get in on the cleaning action and swam happily in the cold water. And the dog needed it. She was starting to stink to high heaven. It felt good to be clean if even only for a short while. And both Brian and Spike had been gentlemen, standing guard with their backs to them.

Yes, they all would be happy to get to the compound or homestead whichever it was, she thought. Maybe there she could repay Brian and Spike by heating them a pot full of water so they too could enjoy a poor man's bath. God knew they deserved it.

They came to a stop on the ridgeline and sat tiredly on the large boulders that were scattered across the flat expanse of the mountain top. Beth laid back over a flat rock and closed her eyes, letting the warmth of the sun relax her. Sarah lay beside her, doing the same. Exhaustion penetrated every muscle in Beth's body, and a sigh escaped her lips. To be done with this trip. To find safety at the compound seemed just a dream. She struggled herself into a sitting position and took a long drink from her bottle of water, grimacing at the bleachy, biting taste. Spike held the binoculars to his eyes and Beth heard him swear softly.

"What do you see?" Brian said. Beth's stomach sank with fear, and she felt Sarah squeeze her hand.

"About twenty of them. Half are on the main trail, the other half heading up."

"How far behind us?"

"Six, maybe seven hours. Those horses won't have an easy a time climbing this bitch. They'll be taking it real slow," Spike replied as he handed the binoculars to Brian.

"Fuck!" Brian swore as he took in the closest group. Handing the binoculars back, he turned to Beth and shook his head. It was time. It was time for him to do what needed doing.

"I'm sorry, Beth. But you ain't gonna like

my plan," he said softly. She scowled and shook her head. She probably wouldn't. Spike looked at Brian, pressed his lips into a hard line, and nodded. They would all do what needed doing. Picking their packs from up off the ground, they all shrugged them back onto sore shoulders. Jessie paced anxiously and whined softly. She sensed the change in mood with her group. Beth reached a hand down and sank her fingers into the dog's fur.

"It's okay girl," she whispered softly. With a mutter of frustration, she fell into step behind Spike. Sarah moved close to her side and grabbed her hand, giving it a tight squeeze. Beth looked at her and smiled. She could see the fear in Sarah's eyes, and it angered her. Why couldn't these people, this Bobby just leave them the fuck alone? Why didn't he just quit already? A burning ember of anger mixed with fear sat like a stone in her stomach.

∞

Brian moved silently, like a ghost through the heavy brush. Every so often he would stop and take a breather, raise his gun, adjust the sight, draw in the distance and then sling it back into the leather rifle hostler on his back. He had one knife tucked into a sheath on his leg; the other rested on his belt.

He thought he left this life of killing behind him. He only wanted to reach home, see his parents, and make his way to settling in this dangerous new world. It seemed though; fate had other ideas. His hands shook with nervous anticipation. There would be death. There would be blood. And, it would come from him. Like a harbinger of doom, he would do the job he needed to do.

Memories of others filled his mind. The screams as he slowly teased the information he needed from their pathetic souls. The cries for mercy as his heart stayed cold and deaf to their whimpering pleas. Shaking his head, he moved ahead. With a hardening of his eyes, he became the killer again.

He didn't know how they found the trail. But he damn sure was going to slow them down. Spike, at his insistence, led Beth and Sarah ahead. He told them not to look back, keep moving forward, and he'd catch up. Beth argued, as he knew she would and he silenced her with one look. The coldness in his eyes brook no argument. These men needed killing. For her and Sarah to survive, they needed to die.

From behind a rocky outcrop, he drew his rifle again. This time he gauged the distance and grinned. Ten men rode their horses in single file climbing a steep and treacherous hill. He drew a breath and took a bead on the lead rider. He calmed his frantic thoughts and eased the anxious trembling of his hands. One tap and he felt the gun slam against his shoulder and watched as the man folded like someone pulled the wind out of him. Smiling, he aimed at the last one in line, one tap and another man down. In quick succession, he took three more before the men could gain their senses and scatter.

Smiling, he muttered. "There, now that evens out the odds just a bit better."

He watched as the remaining men and horses scattered, running full tilt back down the trail they had been climbing. He waited a few minutes then pulling himself up from behind the rock; he slowly made his way down the hill to where the bodies lie.

Chapter Twenty-Five

Harris stared up at the sky through branches that dappled the sunlight. He'd taken a hit. The bullet lodged deep into his shoulder. He slowed his breathing and tried to get up. Finally getting to a sitting position, he looked around and saw four of his men on the ground. Andy, Taylor, Carl, and Doug lie in puddles of blood that was slowly being soaked into the pine needles and sand of the ground. No one was moving. He glanced at his shoulder and saw blood flowing freely from the bullet wound. He tried to move his arm and found it was useless, like a numb hunk of meat just dangling there. He grimaced as the thought of just how fucked he was.

His men had scattered. They'd left him and the others behind. He was sure the cowardly bastards were halfway to Mexico by now. Images of Caitlin floated in his mind. If he died, then Bobby would take her back. And that thought curled his stomach. He loved the woman. He knew she didn't feel the same for him, but that was okay. He treated her nice. Kept her fed and safe. At least as safe as anyone could be in these times.

He heard the crashing in the brush and

looked up to see a large man walking toward him. He tried to stand, tried to pull his sidearm, but dizziness and pain drove him back to the ground.

"Well, well. Lookee here," the man said as he crouched down and placed his forearms across his knees. In one hand he held the biggest blade Harris had ever seen. Harris raised his eyes and what he saw in the other man's gaze sent a chill of horror down his spine.

"Me and you? We're gonna have us a nice little chat," Brian crooned softly, and his lips curved into a cold and deadly smile.

Harris felt his bladder let loose, and he began to cry. As Brian began his nasty work, he sent up a prayer.

"God, forgive me."

He looked down at the man before him. He figured he was about five heartbeats away from death. Blood trickled from the corner of his mouth, sticky and stringy as it hung suspended for a brief second before plopping to the ground. A cold shell formed around his heart. He'd learned all from the man that he could. Taking his knife, he bent his face close to the man's and stared into his eyes. There was not much life left in them. The man choked and gasped as he used his last breath to speak.

"Caitlin," he sighed.

Brian plunged the knife deep into his chest, right over his heart and gave a violent twist. Pulling it out, he wiped the bloody blade across his pant leg. Standing, he stretched his aching back. Killing was hard work. At least the kind of killing he did. His knees popped, sounding like gunshots as he stood. Shit, he was getting too old for this! But, at least now he knew what he was up against; the odds weren't in his favor, but, they were better than he originally thought. This Bobby, he was a dude that needed killing.

From what Harris told him, the horror of what Bobby, his boss, had done and was still doing set Brian's teeth on edge and his eyes hardened with anger as he muttered into the silence surrounding him.

"Yup. He needs killing."

He gathered up three of the horses and tied them single file to each other. On the remaining horse, he emptied the saddlebags and shoved everything into the bags on the horses he would be taking. Having these horses would even out the odds.

Once done, he checked each of the dead men, digging in their pockets for anything he thought would be of value. He grinned in happy surprise as he pulled out from one of the dead men's pockets a tin of Skoal. He opened it to see it was full and taking a pinch between two fingers, he shoved the tobacco between his teeth and his cheek. He then set to work stripping the men of guns, knives, and whatever else he thought would be useful. Taking one last look to be sure he didn't miss anything, he climbed up into the saddle and slowly made his way up the treacherous trail.

As he plodded along, he thought of what Harris had told him. The group that was chasing them was forty strong — led by Bobby, who Harris described as a twisted and evil maniac. Brian learned that Bobby's home base was in a small town in Lee, Massachusetts. Not far from the Appalachian Trail, where there was quick and easy access to all of the small towns that surrounded them.

When the event struck, Bobby moved quickly, gathering up all the men he could find and pulling them into a gang that had easily taken over the town and surrounding areas. Throughout the winter when many were fighting the virus, fighting to stay alive as society began to break down, Bobby and his men went on raids: attacking, killing indiscriminately and building up their supplies by taking from everyone else.

Quickly they accumulated enough supplies and enough firepower to become the most dangerous gang in the area. Then their raids began to extend outward as they built up the drug trade and added human trafficking to their rising business. And sadly, most towns didn't have the defenses nor the manpower to hold them at bay.

Chapter Twenty-Six

Spike heard the pounding of hooves coming up quickly behind them on the trail. Moving swiftly, with his heart in his throat, he grabbed both Beth and Sarah and led them deep into the tangled brush and hid. His heart beat wildly in his chest as he prepared himself. This might be the day he would die, but he would go down fighting. Fear coursed through his veins, not for himself, but for Sarah and Beth. If Bobby's gang got ahold of them, then their lives would be nothing but pain and misery. Short-lived at best. He thought of what he'd told Brian, how it would be a mercy to kill the two before ever letting Bobby take them. He wouldn't be able to do it. He'd die trying to defend them, but he wouldn't be able to kill them.

They'd heard a volley of shot hours earlier and knew it was Brian fighting it out with the men below on the trail. Spike looked over at Beth and saw her lips were pressed firmly together and a determined look glinted in her eyes. She held her rifle at the ready.

"Be ready to run," he whispered.

Beth smiled coldly. There would be no running.

"I mean it, Beth! I will hold them off for as long as I can. You grab Sarah, and you run! You don't know what these men are capable of!" he hissed.

"No!" she argued back, and he saw that as if to back her up, Sarah was shaking her head too. They could run as he said. He would, she knew, hold their attackers off for a few minutes, but that would not be enough. They had horses and would chase her and Sarah down in a matter of seconds. Running, to her, was not an option. Jessie sat nervously beside her and whined softly.

Fearfully she watched through the brush as the horses closed the distance. Her heart beat wildly, her hands shook as she readied her gun and her stomach roiled nauseously. Sarah, beside her, drew her weapon and looked at Beth, nodding. Her crystal blue eyes were wide with fear.

Spike did a touchstone ritual. Gun in one hand, he felt for the knife on his side and the knife strapped to his chest and released each of the metal snaps that held them in place. Sucking in a deep breath, he prepared himself for the fight ahead. He sent up a silent prayer then made the sign of the cross. He'd never been a religious man, but today he thought a little religion couldn't hurt.

As she saw the horses round the bend and Brian sitting tall in the saddle, Beth jumped up in excitement. She squealed as she ran toward him and the three horses he was leading. Spike, letting out a nervous breath, followed along with Sarah and Jessie. As Brian climbed down out of the saddle, Beth threw herself into his arms.

"I thought you were dead! I thought they got you!" she cried as he wrapped his arms around her and held her. Her body trembled with pent up anxiety.

"I heard the gunshots. I thought…." she sobbed in relief. Brian shook his head and grinned, pushing her away to look down into her face. As his eyes met hers, his breath caught in the back of his throat. This woman, this tough, soft, tender, stubborn woman touched his heart as no other before.

"It's okay, Beth. It's okay," he said softly.

Stepping away, she wiped the tears from her face with a shaking hand. Sarah moved up beside her and slung an arm around her shoulder, leaning her head to rest against her. Beth turned her face to Sarah's and smiled through watery eyes.

"We're okay now."

"Dude. Nice to see ya," Spike said, smiling as he reached out and clasped Brian's shoulder with his hand. He looked at the horses with a grin.

"So I take it you got them boys to give up their horses, eh?"

Brian laughed softly. "Yeah, they just handed them on over." He watched Sarah as she moved away from Beth and petted one of the chestnut mares on her nose. This was his family. He let that thought settle with him for a moment, then smiled.

Beth cut him a quizzical look, and he shrugged his shoulders. He thought it best she did not know the details of what happened down in the valley. What would she think of him if she knew how much of a cold-hearted killer he really was? Would she still be happy to see him? Cry tears of relief? Or would it repulse her? No, he would never let her know of the dirty work he was capable of.

"We've got some time so why don't we sit and have a bite to eat and I'll fill you guys in on what I've found out about our friend Bobby," Brian suggested.

They all nodded. Brian pulled up a downed log from the woods and sat. Beth moved in beside him, close enough that their thighs were touching. He reached down and gently squeezed her hand, then released it. This something that was happening between them left him wanting to explore it more. And he would have time to do that sooner or later. He would make sure of that. Jessie lay at their feet, dozing in the sunshine while Sarah and Spike sat opposite on the ground.

When Brian finished filling them in, he

paused for a moment, drinking a soda he'd pilfered from one of the dead men's saddle bags.

"So, at least now we know what we're up against," he said softly.

Spike nodded and sighed deeply.

"Shit. Man, I knew of this gang, but not how strong they'd become," he muttered.

Beth stood up and paced anxiously, her brow wrinkled in thought. Forty men, minus the five that Brian killed. The odds were still thirty-five to four. They would have a slim chance in hell of fighting it out with them.

"So we move faster than they do," she said determinedly. "And hope they don't catch up to us before we reach your grandfather's compound."

Everyone nodded. That was their only option. Try to stay at least one step ahead.

"Okay, let's ride," Brian said as he climbed up into the saddle.

Chapter Twenty-Seven

Bobby took the low road. He split his men, one group off of the AT, covering the side trails. His group moved to the main trail, cutting off onto every trail that led to back roads and highways. They would find those who killed his brother, of that, he had no doubt. There were only so many places they could hide. And with his men scattered about, those places would be few and far between.

His stomach churned nauseously and cramped. It nearly made him double over, he paused and lightly rubbed it thinking it might be something he'd eaten. Whatever it was made him feel shitty. It was hard to concentrate on the road in front of him, and he pulled a ginger ale from his saddlebag, slowly he sipped it as the horse plodded along. He'd been hitting the white stuff frequently and made a promise to himself that he'd back off a bit. The stuff was poison, but oh he so loved the high it gave him. That must be what was giving him all these stomach issues lately. Too many drugs, too much booze, he had to ease back a bit.

His mind wandered back to the night before. Had he gone too far? He let his temper get the best of him. He didn't mean to hurt her so badly, just a little made him feel powerful. But the little had turned into an all-out blind rage. He began to wonder if she would still be alive when he returned home. He'd left Harris' woman, Caitlin, to take care of her. To clean her up and tend to her wounds, but dang, even he was surprised at his level of violence with her last night.

He still tasted her blood on his teeth. He still felt the ghost of her flesh as he pounded her with his fists. Then he'd brought out his knife, and the echo of her screams still lingered in his ears. He'd savaged her. He lost all sense of himself as he let himself do all those things to her that sane men couldn't even imagine. His ears had become deaf to her pleading, her cries, then her whimpers. He shook his head.

"God, you are one sick mother fucker, dude," he muttered to himself. And he knew this to be true. Part of him knew of his descent into madness, into insanity, and that part of him welcomed it with open arms. He let himself get out of control, and he blamed the drugs, he blamed the grief over the death of his brother, and he blamed the stress he was under. He blamed everything but himself. But guilt had a funny way of gnawing at his stomach.

He relaxed in the saddle as the horse he was riding climbed the hilly dirt road. The gentle rocking motion and the warm sunshine lulled him into a state of daydreaming.

Chapter Twenty-Eight

Roger led the group toward the side trail, up Pysons Gap Road. He knew Spike would not stick to the main AT trail. Nope, his grandson would take the less traveled trail that cut across the mountain. He knew exactly in which direction he would go. And that was right into the jaws of the lion. His lower back nagged at him with a dull ache as he shifted his weight in the saddle. His heart was heavy with worry. His grandson weighed heavy on his mind. He watched as Cain moved his horse up beside him.

"Doing okay, Grampa?" Roger grimaced and nodded. The kid had a smart mouth on him, and sometimes he'd just like to smack it.

"Don't you worry about me, boy, I'll run circles around your skinny ass!" he shot back then grinned. He heard Cain laugh softly.

"I know you will, old man," he replied.

The men Spike was after were the gang out of Lee, Massachusetts. Of that, Roger was sure. They'd been having problems with that gang for months now, and he cursed himself for not taking care of that problem sooner. He saw the group of riders coming toward him and his face split into a wide grin. Leading the group was none other than Spike. Nudging his horse with his heel, he sped up to meet him.

Chapter Twenty-Nine

Bobby led his group down Myrtle Street; a cracked, paved road that had seen better days. Houses dotted either side of the street; old Victorians, Capes, and Ranches; yards overgrown with weeds that spilled out onto the street were unkempt and littered with debris. From behind darkened windows, he could feel eyes on him and he motioned for his men to be wary.

He thought it was probably a once nice neighborhood. This is the kind of neighborhood he would not have been welcomed in not that it mattered anymore. Now he could go into any neighborhood. There was no one to stop him. This town looked to him like it would be worth exploring at a later date. Stopping in front of a white Victorian, he spied a man sitting on a rickety lawn chair in front of an open fire.

"Hey, you!" he barked. The man looked up at him with sunken hollow eyes.

"Have you seen any strangers rolling through here lately?"

The man shook his head and went back to tending his fire oblivious to the danger about to befall him.

With a grunt, Bobby dismounted and walked across the high grass toward the man. His stride long and fast.

"Are you sure no strangers have been through here?"

The man once again raised his eyes to Bobby.

"Fuck you want?" he muttered. Bobby smirked and with one swift movement, kicked the chair spilling the man onto the ground. Standing over him, he grinned.

"I asked you a question," he muttered. Scrambling, the man jumped to his feet just as Bobby pulled his gun. Laughing, he looked over his shoulder at his men then back to the man who stood before him.

"Welp?"

The man glared back at him.

"I told you, man, no one has come through here," he muttered angrily. With one quick movement, Bobby shot him in the face and laughed as the man crumpled to the ground. He heard a scream erupt from inside the house and looking up, saw the door swing open and a woman come running out. He gazed at her with a grin. Tall, blonde, leggy… She looked to be in her mid to late thirties.

"Well, well, what have we got here?" he chuckled as the woman ran toward him and threw herself at him in a fit of fury. He grabbed her roughly by the hair and threw her onto the ground. He landed a sharp kick to her stomach and watched in amusement as she gasped for air and gagged. Had he not been in a hurry, he would've taken the time to get to know this woman better, but the mission called. Turning his head, he looked toward the doorway of the house and saw a child of about three standing there in a dirty diaper and crying while it sucked on its thumb. Raising his gun, he aimed and shot. It wouldn't do to leave a child like that, one so young, to fend for itself. The woman on the ground screamed in agony as she realized just what he'd done.

"My baby! What have you done, you animal!" Bobby turned and kicked her solidly in the face, knocking her out.

Motioning to Derek, one of his men, he instructed him to grab her and tie her up.

"We're bringing her with us."

He wasn't about to pass up a chance to add to his brothel, and she was just the type that he knew would sell quickly.

He turned and walked back to his horse and watched as Derek threw the woman across his saddle. With a wave of his hand, he motioned for his men to follow him.

∞

From the top of a long hill, he spied the group of men as they rode toward him. He motioned for his men to hit the woods and he watched from behind a large pine tree.

The group, twenty or so, rode arrogantly up the middle of the road. He turned his head left, his eyes set on a smaller group snaking up the hill from the other direction.

"Mmmmm...what have we got here folks?" he murmured. He pulled a pair of binoculars from his pocket and peered through the lenses. Four riders. Two women, two men. Then something pink caught his eye, and he swore softly as excitement coursed through him.

"You've got to be kidding me?"

"What Bobby, what do you see?" Jose asked. He'd taken up position right behind him. Bobby turned and smiled coldly.

"That's Harris' horse. They got Harris' horse!"

"How' da ya know that?"

"Because of the pink bow on the bridle, you idiot!" Bobby hissed as he danced excitedly. He'd found them — Billy's killers.

It took his mind only a few seconds to connect the dots. Harris must've caught up with the person or persons who killed Billy. There must've been a fight and Harris lost. That is the only way anyone would ever get Rider, his horse, away from him. He loved that horse more than his woman.

Bobby turned to his men and gave them the signal to get ready. His stomach jumped with excitement, and he took several slow, deep breaths as he watched the two groups getting closer and closer to each other. Bringing up his rifle, he aimed at the woman riding Harris' horse. His finger twitched in anticipation. With a hoot of laughter, a scream of excitement, he told his men to open fire.

"Let's rumble, boys!" he yelled as he danced a jig and squeezed the trigger.

Chapter Thirty

Spike led them down onto the dirt road. They made it. Pysons Gap Road. He sighed in relief. It was only a few short miles to the compound from here. They were in the clear. As he brought his horse to a halt, he turned in the saddle and smiled and pointed to the road in front of them and the group of riders advancing. He was not surprised to see his grandfather leading the group but was surprised to see them out and about. He figured they must be doing their daily patrol of the area.

"We've got company," he said, then laughed. Brian, Sarah, and Beth all looked at him in confusion.

"That's my grandfather," Spike announced, grinning as he turned back to the front and kicked his horse gently, setting it into a trot. Brian grinned and turned to Beth, who was smiling widely. His grin turned to horror as he heard the explosion of a gunshot to his left and watched her jump up in her saddle then crumple, falling to the ground as gunshots exploded around them.

He launched himself from his horse and hit the ditch on the opposite side of the road. Drawing his gun, he looked toward the tree line. He could hear Beth's screams as she lay writhing on the ground and a rage of helplessness burned through him. They were surrounded, and he couldn't get to her. Gunshots rang out from both sides of the road.

He watched in horror as both men and horses fell in the onslaught. Scanning the tree line, he aimed and watched as a man tumbled out from behind a large pine tree.

Crawling along the muddy waters of the ditch, he aimed in on another man and pulled the trigger. The bullet hit home, and he watched as the second man fell.

He glanced over, to look for Spike, and saw him lying in the middle of the road. He wasn't moving. His heart raced, and his hands shook. He took a deep breath to steady himself and scanned the woods. Once more, he saw the bright flash of a gun being fired and aimed in on it. The whine of a bullet close to his ear sent him ducking behind the scrub of grass in the ditch and planting his face into the muddy water. He grit his teeth and exploded up, firing and sprinting for Beth.

∞

Beth lay on the ground, stunned. Her hip screamed with burning pain as she stared up at the pale blue sky and watched as clouds floated in and out of her view. She heard screams from both men and horses as the battle raged. They'd ridden head-on into an ambush. Confused, the question of how Bobby and his men found them ached for answer.

She heard Jessie barking wildly then yelping as she fought to protect Sarah. She watched as a large man stabbed Jessie, driving her to the ground, and then grab Sarah, throwing her across his saddle. She screamed in rage and agony, her throat raw with emotion.

She tried to move, tried to reach for the gun at her side, but found her hands wouldn't cooperate. All she could do was listen and watch as the horror unfolded around her. She cut her eyes to the left and saw Spike dance like a puppet as one bullet after another slammed into his body. Crying, with snot dripping from her nose and trickling down her face, she struggled to move as helplessness filled her.

As sudden as it began, it stopped, and silence filled the air. Men and horses littered the ground. The shooting stopped, and all that remained were the moans of the injured and dying. Brian knelt beside her. Bending, he pulled her into his arms, and his heart exploded in silent agony as he held her to him. She looked up into his face, and tears rolled in fat droplets from her eyes.

"You promise me," she said between hitching, bubbly breaths, "You promise me you will get Sarah back."

Brian nodded. He would get Sarah back, even if it meant traveling to the ends of the earth and killing a thousand men; he would get Sarah back.

"I promise, Beth." He whispered as he buried his face into her soft, auburn hair and held her tight. He could feel the anger singing in his veins, white and hot as it ripped through him.

Chapter Thirty-One

Roger climbed out of the gutter, holding his arm as blood flowed down it; dripping off of the end of his fingers, leaving a trail of bright red droplets on the ground. His ears rang with the echoes of gunshots now gone silent. Stunned, he gazed around. What just happened?

Men and horses littered the road. His eyes landed on Spike who lay prone in the road, writhing and twisting like some garish puppet being tugged on by an unseen hand. Dragging himself into a run, he crossed the road and kneeled over his grandson. His heart exploded in fear.

"Spike! Spike!" he yelled as he pulled at him with his good hand. His voice sounded like it was coming from an echo chamber.

"Grampa?" Spike choked as he moaned in pain. "I'm fine, help me sit up."

Roger shook his head. He'd seen the bullets slamming into him. He wasn't fine.

"No, son. Stay still; you've been shot."

Spike winced then grinned. Yes, he'd been shot. Several times. Reaching a hand up, he tapped on his chest and coughed and then moaned and grimaced. His chest felt like a troop of dancers just tapped danced across it.

"Bulletproof vest, Grampa. You know I'd never leave home without it…ouch!"

Roger shook his head. He didn't know whether to hug him or kill him.

"Fuck boy! I thought you were a goner!" he said, then smiled as he used his good arm to help him up off the pavement.

Once standing and steady, they both took a look around. Spike saw Brian kneeling over Beth who lay on the ground and his breath caught in his throat as his heart plummeted to his gut. Rushing over, he knelt beside him while Roger went to assess the damage to his own group of men.

"How bad?" he asked.

"Bad. She needs a doctor. Like now." Brian replied, his voice cracking with panic. He held a folded-up shirt tightly to her stomach, applying pressure. There was so much blood. His hands were covered with it, and it was still pouring from her as if someone turned on a faucet.

Roger came slowly walking toward them, shaking his head. He had four of his men dead and two wounded. He instructed his men to begin loading them onto the horses and get them back to the compound.

What happened? Who ambushed them? He stopped beside Spike and looked down at the woman on the ground. Blood pooled underneath her and formed a garish puddle near her left hip.

Her lips, he noticed, had a distinct bluish tinge which told him she was losing ground fast.

"We have a doctor in the compound. Get her loaded up and be quick about it or she ain't gonna make it."

Spike gently lifted Beth to the horse Brian was sitting atop. She moaned softly. Brian held her tightly against his chest. Looking down at Spike, he cut his eyes to the ditch.

"Bring Jessie. She's been stabbed."

Spike nodded.

"Sarah?"

"They've got her, man. They got her," Brian hissed, his eyes filling with pain. Spike felt his heart plummet.

"We'll get her back. You can bet on that, my friend!" he growled.

Chapter Thirty-Two

Brian looked coldly off into the distance. His eyes saw nothing and everything. He tucked the knife into his waistband. A cold and dead calm settled over him. Reaching down, he stroked a warm hand across Jessie's head.

It had been one week since the ambush. Jessie had healed well and now was ready to travel. The doctor at the compound, Zeke, operated on Beth then sedated her heavily. The bullet was lodged deep into her hip, shattering the bone. She'd lost so much blood that for days they all had doubts that she would survive. But she was a fighter; he'd give her that. She hung on.

Through many long hours, he sat by her bed while Lori, one of the nurses at the compound, checked in every few hours and changed her bandages, adjusted her I.V.s and gave her more medication. She did her best to keep her as comfortable as possible. On the fourth day she finally opened her eyes, and Brain knew the danger passed. It felt as though a great weight was lifted from his heart.

He stood tiredly and stretched. Looking at Lori, he motioned for her to follow him out of the room.

"I'm going for a walk," he said. She smiled and nodded. He'd been by Beth's side for the past four days, and she thought it was high time he took a break. She envied Beth in that she had a man who cared for her as deeply as this man did.

He walked slowly through the compound. His eyes were taking in every detail. He whistled softly, impressed with set up that Roger had going. The compound consisted of several outbuildings; a clinic, aka makeshift hospital, a common cafeteria, a common shower facility, and a large building for meetings, worship, and anything else they needed it for.

There were also small, efficiency homes, about one hundred total. Up high there were towers with platforms, constantly manned with armed guards. The perimeter of the complex heavily fortified — a series of ditches filled with coiled barbed wire, followed by more barbed wire fencing. A few yards in, away from the ditches, ran another line of defense, this time more medieval. A wall of spiked sticks sharp enough to impale horse or man ran the entire length of the perimeter. It was medieval and efficient.

This Roger, he thought smiling, damn sure didn't fool around when it came to defending his own. These defenses were some very serious business. He was sure there were even more nasty surprises that he wasn't seeing.

As he walked, he thought of Sarah, and his heart hurt with the pain of knowing that monster Bobby had her. His hands shook with rage as he thought of what that pig might be doing to her and he swore, by all that was holy, he'd make that man pay for every pain he might be causing her.

He'd made himself wait until Beth was out of the woods before leaving to fulfill his promise to her of finding and bringing Sarah back. She was now stable, and he was anxious to leave. Anxious to go and right a wrong. Sighing deeply, his mind made up; he walked back to the hospital.

He entered the room and sat beside the bed. He smiled as Beth opened her eyes and gazed into his.

"I'm going to get our girl back," he said softly.

Beth nodded. "You bring her back to me, Brian, and while you're at it, make sure you come back in one piece as well," she whispered weakly.

Chapter Thirty-Three

"Well, girl. It's time we go hunting. Let's go get our girl back, okay?" he murmured. The dog growled softly as if in reply. He climbed up into the saddle and kicked the horse gently. He had become the killer again; it was time to go to work. Hearing a cough from behind him, he turned in the saddle.

"I work alone," he growled.

"Sorry buddy, where you go, I go," Spike said, then laughed as he saw Brian's scowl.

"Yeah buddy, ain't this gonna be some shit show fun!" Spike said then hooted with laughter. He had a score of his own to settle. If it weren't for Bobby, his wife and sons would still be alive. Yeah, the man hadn't killed them with his hand, but the men who worked for him did and the way Spike figured it, he was as much to blame as the dead man with his throat slit lying out on the trail.

Yes, he had a score to settle. And, he had a certain, sweet little blue-eyed girl to rescue, one with a beautiful smile and a bad attitude. And he had a friend who needed his back watched, whether or not the arrogant bastard would ever admit to it.

"Just shut up and ride," Brian growled.

The cop and the killer. Shaking his head, Spike chuckled as he kicked his horse gently and sank into the rhythm of her gentle gait.

If you've enjoyed this book, then keep watch for the next story in this series, Valley of Vengeance. The journey continues. One fraught with the perils of this new landscape as new friends are met, and new enemies are around every corner.

Valley of Vengeance:

Brian made a promise.
A simple mission to rescue Sarah has turned into one of the most dangerous journeys of his life. He finds himself torn between rescuing Sarah and setting out for safer grounds or standing strong and taking on one of the most dangerous gangs in the North East.

About the Author:

N.A. Broadley lives in New Hampshire, on the homestead where she stays prepared. She lives a simple life, surrounded by family and friends.

Writing has always been a passion, and she's grateful for the time and opportunity to engage in activities that allow her the pleasure of following that passion.

Join her in The Written Apocalypse and Women of The Apocalypse, two great Facebook groups for more exciting books and releases from many great authors. A place to chat, swap stories, and keep up on the latest and the greatest.

https://www.facebook.com/groups/writtenapocalypse/

https://www.facebook.com/groups/WomenoftheApocalypse/